Alabama Irish

Center Point
Large Print

Also by James Russell Lingerfelt
and available from Center Point Large Print:

The Mason Jar

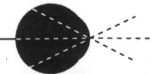

**This Large Print Book carries the
Seal of Approval of N.A.V.H.**

Alabama Irish

James Russell Lingerfelt

CENTER POINT LARGE PRINT
THORNDIKE, MAINE

This Center Point Large Print edition is published in
the year 2016 by arrangement with the author.
Published in association with MacGregor Literary, Inc.

The text of this Large Print edition is unabridged.
In other aspects, this book may vary
from the original edition.
Printed in the United States of America
on permanent paper.
Set in 16-point Times New Roman type.

ISBN: 978-1-68324-210-9

Library of Congress Cataloging-in-Publication Data

Names: Lingerfelt, James Russell, author.
Title: Alabama Irish / James Russell Lingerfelt.
Description: Center Point Large Print edition. | Thorndike, Maine :
Center Point Large Print, 2016.
Identifiers: LCCN 2016040267 | ISBN 9781683242109
    (hardcover : alk. paper)
Subjects: LCSH: Large type books.
Classification: LCC PS3612.I5525 A78 2016 | DDC 813/.6—dc23
LC record available at https://lccn.loc.gov/2016040267

TABLE OF CONTENTS

If you can keep your head when all about you
Are losing theirs and blaming it on you,
If you can trust yourself when all men doubt
    you,
But make allowance for their doubting too;
If you can wait and not be tired by waiting,
Or being lied about, don't deal in lies,
Or being hated, don't give way to hating,
And yet don't look too good, nor talk too wise:

If you can dream—and not make dreams
    your master;
If you can think—and not make thoughts
    your aim;
If you can meet with Triumph and Disaster
And treat those two impostors just the same;
If you can bear to hear the truth you've spoken
Twisted by knaves to make a trap for fools,
Or watch the things you gave your life to,
    broken,
And stoop and build 'em up with worn-out
    tools:

If you can make one heap of all your winnings
And risk it on one turn of pitch-and-toss,
And lose, and start again at your beginnings

And never breathe a word about your loss;
If you can force your heart and nerve and
    sinew
To serve your turn long after they are gone,
And so hold on when there is nothing in you
Except the Will which says to them: "Hold
    on!"

If you can talk with crowds and keep your
    virtue,
Or walk with Kings—nor lose the common
    touch,
If neither foes nor loving friends can hurt you,
If all men count with you, but none too much;
If you can fill the unforgiving minute
With sixty seconds' worth of distance run,
Yours is the Earth and everything that's in it,
And—which is more—you'll be a Man, my
    son!

"If—" by Rudyard Kipling

Alabama Irish

Chapter 1

August 5, 1998

Uncle Mike said I should start keeping a journal to exercise "reflection and introspection" and talk about my fears, because once I've written them down and they're in front of me, I will be able to face them. I had to go look up "introspection" in the dictionary.

He said we spend so much time analyzing others that we never give a lot of attention to what's going on inside us. He said writing in a journal would be kind to me, and I like that, because I don't believe there's a lot of kindness in the world. I see people in it just for themselves.

Apparently, it's supposed to be like I'm writing letters to a friend. I've never really had a lot of friends, so this whole thing will be new to me. I'm not going to tell anyone that my journal is my friend. People think I'm weird enough as it is. They really do.

I'm seventeen, I'm about to begin my senior year of high school, and my name is Brian Bailey. I don't like to think about my past a lot. It wasn't a fun past. I don't give too much thought to the future either, because honestly, I'm not sure I'll live very long. And my greatest fear is that one day I'll become just like my parents. My mom's a crackhead, always blaming me for everything, and I've never met my dad.

Uncle Mike said when I become an old man and my memory is gone, I'll have my journals to tell me about the life I lived. And if I have kids, they might enjoy reading about me. I get that. If I have kids, I don't want them growing up thinking I've always been just an old fogey.

I asked him if I could cuss in my journal, and he said maybe I shouldn't because you never know who might read it one day. He said I'd regret the profanity and wish I had just used regular language. I asked him if I should worry about run-on sentences and grammar and punctuation and stuff like that, because last year my English teacher was on me all the time about it.

She even said not to begin a sentence with the word "and." But my argument is that that's how people talk. Besides, who comes up with all these rules anyway? Honor versus honour, when to use "me" or "I" or "myself." Someone, some person or some people, had to come up with all these rules a long time ago, didn't they? So can they say what a rule is and I can't?

Anyway, I shared all this with Uncle Mike and he said that wasn't his point. But maybe I shouldn't get too liberal with how I write because "Practice produces habit, and habit produces character." That's an Aristotle quote that Uncle Mike makes his fighters memorize.

I pointed out that cuss words are really just words our ancestors decided to call profane. Words are just symbols to describe what's going on inside us. I read that in a *Men's Health Magazine* article where a college professor was interviewed. I was at Buster's barber shop and it was a magazine on the table that holds up the lamp that no one ever turns on.

I read a lot of *Men's Health*, and I really like the sex articles. They teach you how to be a good lover and I hope to be that one day for my wife. I think every guy wants his girl to say he was the best lover ever. Uncle Mike and Aunt Karen think I read them for the diet and weight training, and I do, but the sex articles are what I always go to first.

Anyway, Uncle Mike said I need to be sensitive to cultural "mores." And then I had to go and look up what the word "more" means. It means customs or traditions of people living in communities. So far, I've already started lots of sentences with the word "and." And no one can do anything about it.

I asked Uncle Mike if I should write about my mom and Darren. I don't like Mom, but Darren was my best friend. He was also my brother. Uncle Mike said yes. When I began another question, he said I was making this too complicated, and maybe I should just write whatever I want. He was pretty frizzled or frazzled, whatever that word is, and he looked like he wanted to beat his head against the wall. So I dropped it.

Uncle Mike and Aunt Karen aren't my real aunt and uncle. I just call them that. I came to live with them after I left Mom's house and after Grandmother died. I live with them in a two bedroom house in a poorer neighborhood, but it's not too poor.

There's lots of asphalt around us and not a lot of kids play outside after the sun goes down. But I don't mind. It beats the trailer park I grew up in. Uncle Mike and Aunt Karen's two sons shared a room, and when they grew up they both graduated from the University of Alabama. Now they head their own families and are doing well. Uncle Mike and Aunt Karen did have three sons, but their first son, Tommy, got leukemia when he was four years old and died.

Uncle Mike graduated from West Point in philosophy and military tactics, then he served as a major in the Marine Corps. Later, he opened a boxing dojo in Tuscaloosa. When Mixed Martial Arts got popular, and Uncle Mike saw boxers turning, he hired a guy from Atlanta's MMA scene. Then, Uncle Mike took basic classes in Muay Thai and Brazilian Jiu Jitsu to better understand everything.

"They're good people," Grandmother said. Most grandmothers would keep their kids away from the MMA scene, but I think Grandmother knew that if I didn't get involved in something and get myself a mentor, I'd get into trouble. I grew up in West Blocton, which is "across the railroad tracks." That means trouble. Social services could set up three or four centers there and people in town would still come looking for handouts. The entire town isn't like that, but once you cross the tracks, you're in a completely different world.

Growing up, the air was always filled with the smell of fresh-cut grass or burning plastic. People still burn their garbage there. They can't afford to pay the city to haul it away.

Anyway, Mike's Dojo was famous. Kids at school talked about how Uncle Mike's fighters made it to national championships. I remember shaking Uncle Mike's hand for the first time when I was thirteen or so. We were in Grandmother's yard. He stopped by on a Saturday. Uncle Mike is stocky with a dad's belly and a square jaw and gray hair at his temples. That day he didn't smile or frown, at least not at first. He probably wondered if I would be trouble to him in the long run.

I looked down at the ground, which is something I never did to anyone. I thought I had to be tough and strong, and that meant looking people in the eye and not letting anyone see any weakness in me. I hoped he'd be different than the coaches at school. They always just gave you the stare down because they didn't want you to cause them any trouble.

"After school," Uncle Mike said, "you'll come to the dojo and help out. All right?" Then he placed his hands on his hips and grinned at me. "I can tell by looking at you that you'll be great. Might even make a great fighter one day." Looking back, he was probably just saying all that. But I loved hearing that come from him, a leader and hero in the community, and that's how I came to work for him.

On Saturdays, I worked at the dojo from nine to five, and then full-time during the summers. He paid me minimum wage and told Grandmother to put it into a savings account for me. I mopped, swept, cleaned, and greased the weight machines. I watched the fighters train and spar. I'd lean on the ropes or the cage, seeing it all in real life for the first time. Uncle Mike let it slide every now and then, and then he'd shout across the gym, "Brian! That work won't get done by itself!"

After my chores, Uncle Mike would let me hold up the mitts for the fighters to punch while he trained others in cardio and core strength. In all the years I've worked for Uncle Mike, I've never fought in competitions, but I did start sparring in the cage when I was fifteen. Even with padded gloves and pulled punches, we'd bloody each other's noses. I learned the kicks and locks and often used them on trainees, to introduce them to it, but it was also to test myself.

I became friends with the fighters, though they all had graduated high school and some of them were already grandparents. One of the fighters, Tony, became my good friend. He's old enough to be my dad, but he isn't the sharpest tool in the shed, as Uncle Mike likes to say. For Christmas two years ago Tony gave me a rubber hose as long as my forearm with a steel bolt shoved into its end. He said now that I was learning to drive, it can be my billy club to keep in the truck in case "some low-life try to do ye hawm." I hid it under Uncle Mike's driver's seat. It's still there.

There are more stories I want to write, but I don't want to right now. Uncle Mike said the longer we wait to write our own stories, the more we forget, and that gets worse with age. So I know I'll get to the important stories real soon.

I would write about Darren, making sure to include all the good times we had. But if I think about him too much, I'll get sad. And I'm trying to be more happy. Because we become happy by "letting our minds dwell on the positive."

I hope nobody reads this. I don't want to sound like a pansy. It's late, so I'm going to bed.

Goodnight!

BB

• • •

August 7, 1998

I'm not looking forward to going back to school next week. It's my senior year, and the only nice part is that I'm graduating soon. I go to Tuscaloosa County High School. The summer's been too nice, working with fighters who like me. I want people at school to like being around me, but I think it's hard for them, really. I hate high school, though I never tell anyone that.

I don't trust the kids there no matter how much I want to. I really tried hard to make friends when I transferred from middle school. The kids I knew back then either went onto different high schools, or they moved away, got into trouble with the law, or their moms didn't want them hanging around me.

It's okay. I got into trouble with the sheriff my freshman year and everyone found out about it. It's a long story, but the short version is that I was fifteen and I was running around with some boys from bad homes. Uncle Mike kept asking me why I didn't have friends my age, so I looked for friends who were like me. They weren't naive and sheltered like the rest of them.

Anyway, they had parents who didn't care what they did as long as they weren't in the way. We broke some streetlights and painted graffiti on tunnels over roads and stuff. Then, one night, a few of us were playing poker at a guy's house on a Friday night.

During the game, one of the boys had this great idea that we could "borrow" a poker table from the country club, where his dad was a manager. The club was closed, and I stayed in the truck while they went in using a hidden key. When they returned, one of the boys was carrying a cash box. As soon as they started toward the car, sheriff lights flashed. The sheriff accused me of being the lookout. But that wasn't true at all. I was just waiting.

The sheriff said, "Those boys need to be taught early." So I have a criminal record, guilty by association. I kind of got that sheriff back though. Every Thursday night he'd be at the donut shop in Northport. I mean, what a genius. You're a law enforcement guy and a teenager knows your schedule? No wonder they need guns.

I waited for him under his sheriff car. And when he stepped to the car door with his coffee and donut, I lit a line of fire crackers behind the driver's side tire. I rolled out the other side and hid behind a street corner.

One of the kids, Scottie, who got in trouble with me over the cash box, he was in the bushes videoing the whole thing. Those firecrackers rattled and that sheriff started dancing, and he dropped his donut and spilled his coffee all over his shirt because he didn't know whether to jump, dive, or draw his gun.

After about three seconds, he hid behind a tree and finally realized the difference between gun shots and firecrackers. Man, if it had been real gunfire he'd been killed. And boy, was his face red hot. I think it really embarrassed him too, because people were running outside to see what all the ruckus was. I know I didn't really pay him back because I can't give him a criminal record.

When someone is trying to intimidate me or dominate me, I just can't take it. I look for ways to stand my ground and get them back. Uncle Mike says it's because of insecurities I developed as a kid, especially after what happened to Darren, but I don't know. I know lots of people who don't let others pick on them.

Anyway, like I was saying, by the time I got to high school, most kids would drop any friend that didn't make them look popular. And it seems like it's just getting worse. They'll actually drop friends who make uncool remarks. I'll watch them give each other three strikes. You say something uncool, you can get by with it once. Second time is a warning, and you see that by the way they start giving each other the cold shoulder. Third time, you're out.

When I started high school, I met some girls and paid them some attention. They're pretty and smell real nice, but most I've met are immature, too wrapped up in image and money and who their circles of friends are. I used to go to football games because Uncle Mike said I should.

It's the cool place to go on Friday nights, but I'd always sit by myself at the bottom of the bleachers, so I stopped going because I didn't like the way it made me feel. Besides, hanging out by yourself like that at a high school football game will turn the girls away real quick. Which of them wants to run around with a boy that even boys don't want to hang out with?

It probably doesn't help matters that last year, when I was a junior, I got into a fight with Jake, the captain of the wrestling team. He's also the starting quarterback on the football team. Yeah, getting on the bad side of a guy like that isn't the best thing in the world.

I'm 5'10" without my shoes, and I weigh a lean 155 pounds with my clothes off. So I look and move like I'm athletic, but I don't wrestle or play football or basketball or soccer or baseball, and I'm not in the marching band, and I'm not a geek or in the student government, and I'm not an emo or a goth kid who wears black from head to toe, and I'm not a skateboarder. And I'm not a druggie. I'm an MMA fighter. So that makes me a bit of a misfit I guess. I just keep to myself, mostly. And that makes people think I'm weird.

I've also had a shaved head ever since I can remember. It's easier that way. Guys my age are always putting gel in their hair and trying to look good for all the girls. I've also worn black t-shirts every day since I was eight years old. It's my way of flipping off the kids across the tracks who wear spotless white t-shirts all the time and think they're cool. Darren would laugh if he knew I wore black. That's another reason why we were best friends. We didn't like to follow crowds. We created our own paths.

Anyway, I think the effects of all that, when no one knows a lot about you, and when they realize you don't care what they think of you, when you don't care about being their friend, you become a bit of a novelty item. And that attracts attention. And when a rumor surfaces that you have been trained to fight at Mike's Dojo, and you even help train the fighters, well, that opens up all kinds of questions. The bullies want to test you. Is it out of fear or curiosity? I'm not sure. Maybe both.

I had P.E. with some of the football players/wrestlers, and we all dressed in the same locker room. Some of them were talking about Mike's Dojo. One day they joked that I was probably the janitor.

Jake, a head taller than me, was bigger than almost everyone, and he had dark hair, squints for eyes, and a chiseled chin that drove the girls crazy. He was one of those guys who could be funny in the mean sort of way. And he had his groupies or cronies or entourage or whatever the right word is. They were like a bunch of hyenas, laughing at everything he said and did. I didn't like them.

"You know how to fight?" Jake asked me with a grin, while hanging his shirt in one of the lockers. He glanced around and his five or six pals were smiling at me and then at him, keeping their eyes on him while watching me out of the corners of their eyes. I guess they thought I was too stupid to know what they were doing.

A handful of the younger students were dressing fast. They hadn't really gone through puberty yet and they didn't want to get in the middle of anything. It's hard to be in the locker room when you're young and small.

I had already put on my black tee and jeans, and I remember feeling my heart pounding and my hands and feet turning numb. I hate feeling like a target. I do remember most of the fight. I didn't black out like they claim you do in the movies, but things got hazy until the fight was over. Basically, Jake and his friends picked a fight, and I broke Jake's nose, cracked one of his ribs, and a kid standing in the corner told me later that two of Jake's friends had to drag me off him.

Jake and his pals hadn't understood yet that kings of jungles aren't the largest animals or the quickest. It's all about the size of the fight in the animal, right? I mean, if size mattered, the elephant would be king, not the lion.

Later, I felt really bad about it. And even though it was self-defense, the principal told Uncle

Mike that if I got into another fight, I'd be kicked out of school. The last thing the school needs is a trained fighter breaking bones and cracking ribs of their star athletes. I mean, they had to take Jake to the hospital. I haven't talked to those boys since. Jake sees me in the halls every now and then and never looks me in the eye. But he knows I'm there. You know when someone knows you're there and they're doing their best not to look at you.

I haven't been in another fight since, but no one's tried to mess with me, either. I catch people staring at me every now and then, even though a year has passed, like I'm some kind of freak. Or they glance at me and don't want me to notice. Though it didn't do me any good in my social life, it sent a message to people about bullies. If you hit a bully as hard as you can, and you keep hitting him, he might get the best of you and win. But he won't pick on you after that. Bullies like easy targets. That's why they're called bullies and not fighters.

It's not like in the movies where hitting the bully just makes it worse and he eventually kills you. When someone dies on the streets in real life, it's usually over money.

I'm tired now and I have school tomorrow, so I need to go to bed.

Goodnight!

BB

• • •

August 18, 1998

School's going okay, and I'm trying to make the best of it. The cafeteria food is pretty bad so I bring my own lunch. The lunchroom ladies let me keep my lunch in the kitchen fridge. I'm friends with them because they heard about my life in elementary school and how those other lunchroom ladies had to feed me breakfast every morning. They treat me nicer than they treat anyone else.

I always bring beef or chicken with a bowl of avocado mixed with walnuts, pecans, and cashews. That's for proteins and oils. I feel sorry for people who have to eat lunchroom food. The pizza is like cardboard and shaped like a stop sign. The fruit cups are mixed fruit from a can, and every piece of the fruit tastes exactly the same. I mean, you can eat a grape, but it tastes just like the cantaloupe. The sloppy joe? I'm still unsure about what kind of meat it really is.

I'm doing okay in school in health and English class, but terrible in the others. I do just enough to pass, and that's good enough for me. I'll never leave the dojo. Even if I do, I'll just open one up on my own. I do like English class, though. I read excerpts from George Washington's resolutions about all the stuff he believed in doing, like using good table manners and not reading the newspaper in the company of friends. But then I learned he wrote them when he was thirteen years old and I lost all interest.

We read some stuff by Marcus Aurelius and he said that a mature person doesn't give into fits of anger and passion. That mildness and gentleness are more agreeable. I found that interesting since he was a Roman ruler who killed millions of people.

Anyway, I like learning from books that are actually fun to read. I didn't finish reading Washington's stuff, and I got in trouble for it. When the teacher asked why I didn't read it, I said I didn't care too much for what a thirteen-year-old boy had to say about manners when he lived 200 years ago. So she's letting me read *Walden* by Thoreau. And I like it much better.

There's a desk here in my room that belonged to Uncle Mike's sons. I write here sometimes, and sometimes on my bed. When I want to think, I go to the window or the back deck and look up at the moon. I like to think there.

Sometimes I watch the moon and think about all the people in the entire history of people who also looked up at that very same moon. And I think about how they all saw sunsets and sunrises of the very same sun I see, and that they enjoyed all those streaks of colors. That one moon and one sun unite the entire human race. I think that's really cool.

Goodnight!

BB

• • •

August 19, 1998

My journal is just notebook paper in a three-ring binder. That way I can add paper to it as I go along. Right now I'm writing at my desk, and it's beside the window because I moved it, and I can see the crape myrtles in the yard. Robins and squirrels and bluebirds nest in them. They're peaceful to watch, even though I can still hear the traffic in front of our house.

Today, I was holding the punching bag for Tony. That's always a good time to talk to Tony because the workouts free his mind and he's not afraid to tell me stuff. Tony is past his prime and doesn't fight anymore, but he likes to stay in shape.

I told him what Uncle Mike wants me to do with the journal, but I said it with a laugh because I didn't want Tony to make fun of me. You know, laugh at yourself before someone else does. But he said it was a good idea and maybe he should do it, too. But it'll be hard for him because he said he's dyslexic. He said it's when you see words and letters backwards.

I told Tony he didn't seem retarded, and he said dyslexic doesn't mean retarded, and that I need to be careful who I use the word "retarded" around. Because they might get offended. I don't like to offend people because I don't want to make enemies, but just because someone is offended doesn't mean they're right. I asked him what word I should use instead, and he said "mentally disabled" because now "mentally handicapped" offends people. I can't keep up.

Tony is a real cool guy. I like him a lot. He's black and I've been told not to call black people black, but to call them African American. Because being called black offends black people. But not all people with black skin are from Africa. Some of them are from Jamaica. And some are from South America. I know because I've seen them on TV.

So I'm not really sure why black people want all black people to be called African Americans. I'm white and I don't mind people calling me white. I don't ask people to call me Irish American or German American or Native American–American even though Grandmother said we're part Cherokee. I've even had black people call me a cracker, but I thought it was clever and funny, so I laughed. I guess it's like Uncle Mike says. It's all about how you choose to respond. That says a lot about where you are in your journey.

I guess you could say we all came from Africa at some point. So really, maybe all of us are African American. In class, we read this book called *The Journey of Man* and the author said we all came from a woman in East Africa about 65,000 years ago. That research was based on

DNA strands. The author was an atheist, but he didn't believe we came from monkeys.

He's the first atheist I've ever heard of who didn't believe we came from monkeys. But I've noticed when I pull my ears forward so they're sticking out perpendicular, and I tighten my lips and push air into my cheeks so that they blow up, and I cross my eyes, I look like a monkey.

Tony is in his forties. I don't know if he's African American or not. But he showed me moves he learned from fighting on the streets, like hiding a roll of quarters in your fist when you punch someone. Push on those pressure points behind their ears and at the ridge of their noses. He even passed along spy tricks like sticking a rolled piece of paper between your doorjamb and door, but a few inches up from the ground, so if someone goes into your house when you're not there, you'll see the paper lying on the floor when you come back.

Aunt Karen is making salmon patties tonight, and I'm really excited. I can smell them now. It's canned salmon with the bones removed. She adds flour, milk, eggs, onions, garlic, corn meal and lemon juice and then she churns it up and flattens them out and fries them in vegetable oil. Kind of like a crab cake. They're delicious.

I'm tired and hungry, so that's all.

Goodnight!

BB

• • •

November 5, 1998

I turned eighteen yesterday! Uncle Mike and Aunt Karen gave me a subscription to *Men's Health Magazine* for my birthday because that's what I asked for. We ate cake and ice cream, but I didn't eat more than half a cup. I don't think they would have minded me eating an entire bowl like they did, but I have really good abs right now and I don't want to ruin them. I have a six pack, and sometimes when I'm training real hard and running hills all the time, I can count eight.

Uncle Mike wanted to tell the fighters about my birthday but I asked him not to because I didn't want them giving me gifts. I didn't want them spending money because a lot of them can't afford it. How they can afford a membership at the dojo, I don't know. Most of them drive cars that I'm surprised still run. But Uncle Mike said the dojo is their family and their release from stress and a place to call home. And he can't give memberships for free because people would take advantage of it. Besides, he still has to make a living.

The dojo really is like a home. When Uncle Mike walks into the dojo, men stop what they're doing and shake his hand. Some even hug him like he's an uncle or something. He's helped many men from abusive and broken homes. Aunt

Karen said he helps them see the good in their lives and in the lives of others.

He can get on my nerves sometimes, though. He's always running his mouth, but in a good way. He doesn't talk down at people. That's what I mean. Anyway, he runs his mouth in the weight room and in the truck when we're riding somewhere, and even at the dinner table at home. Preaching.

Uncle Mike doesn't have sons or military boys to teach anymore. So he pours into me and his fighters. He started pouring into me even before I came to live with them. Uncle Mike and Aunt Karen invited me over for lunch on Sundays, and Uncle Mike would teach me chess. "If you play chess," he'd say, "you learn to plan ahead. To know where you're going. It trains you to think like that. Use your past to guide you. Not bind you."

He always likes to point out that no one can make me angry. That's a reaction I choose. Nobody can make me offended. I choose to be offended. And that when we're emotional, the emotional side of the brain heats up and out-shouts the logical side. That's why people can fly off the handle and lose their temper, and then have major regrets about it later.

But Uncle Mike also knows about the scary fight I got into when I was in middle school, so I understand him always preaching at me. It was

31

scary because I flipped out. Back when I was eleven, I was at a Halloween party, and this was three years after Darren died.

Derek, a kid from class, invited me because I think he felt sorry for me. It wasn't his party. The boy hosting it was homeschooled or something. I was sleeping in dugouts on the baseball field back then because I didn't want to go home and hear Mom cussing at me. Also, her boyfriends would beat on me. This was before I went to live with Grandmother.

Anyway, we were at the party and all the moms were in the other room, laughing and talking. But this boy, about a foot taller than me, he walked in wearing a hockey mask. He was the host's cousin. I can't explain why my body reacted this way, but when I saw that boy wearing that hockey mask, a sweat broke out all over me, I felt my heart race, and my knees started trembling. I didn't feel it as strong when I faced Jake years later, but it was there, deep inside.

I was scared to death of that boy in the mask, and it made me furious. I felt sick to my stomach, and my lungs felt all squeezed. I mean, that mask really freaked me out. "Take that mask off!" I screamed. And when he didn't, I swung at him to slap that mask off, and I hit it, but it didn't fly off because it was tied on with one of those elastic strings. It just swung to the side of his face. He shoved me, and then that was it.

I pounced on him like a Comanche. I beat his head with my fists. He was covering his face, but I kept swinging. Just one giant fury. He fell to the ground and then I got on top of him and I kept working him. I made his left eyebrow swell up and made his nose bleed. Three screaming moms pulled me off him.

I'll never forget the look on all the moms' faces. Like I was some kind of freak. That one mom grabbed my arm and squeezed it where the bicep meets the elbow. "What do you think you're doing?" she screamed. Who did she think she was, I thought, talking to me like that and squeezing my arm. I jerked away from her. "You don't care about me," I yelled.

The mom of the kid who invited me took me home. Looking back, I feel sorry for her. She was embarrassed in front of her friends. She asked me to sit in the front seat while her son, my classmate who invited me, sat in the back. I think she just wanted to keep an eye on me.

When we got to Grandmother's, I turned to her, reached behind my seat and patted her son's knee. I told her, "If you don't tell anyone what happened, there won't be any problems at school. Derek and I will get along just fine." Then I looked back at him and nodded. "Friends for life."

Maybe I was a freak, but it worked. That mom didn't say a word. When I stepped out of the car, she was already driving off before I could even close the car door.

A week passed and I was feeling all horrible and all. Derek was still nice to me when he saw me in the halls, but he kept his distance and didn't want to talk much. I told him to tell the boy that I was sorry for what I did, and to tell the moms too, but I don't know if he ever did.

I didn't mean to hurt that kid. I tried to make myself cry when I got home, but I couldn't. For some reason, I haven't cried since Darren's funeral.

I watched *Old Yeller* at Uncle Mike's and Aunt Karen's, and I didn't cry. *Where The Red Fern Grows*? I watched it, and I didn't cry. And a lot of grown men cry at the end of *Field of Dreams*, but not me. I know because Uncle Mike's friends were visiting from out of town, and they were leaving the room to cry. One of them even said he had something in his eye. I kid you not. Like anyone would believe that.

People also cry at the end of *It's A Wonderful Life*. Especially when George's brother says, "To my big brother George, the richest man in town." It comes on TV every Christmas. And every Christmas, we watch it. And I don't cry. But Uncle Mike cries.

Every time.

Then he'll go into the kitchen and fix himself a bowl of ice cream. To freeze those tears, I guess.

I don't know what's wrong with me sometimes. Why can't I be like everyone else?

BB

November 6, 1998

Aunt Karen is cooking dinner and it smells so good! She cooks stuff like pinto beans, turnip greens, and broiled chicken or hamburger steak. Every lunch and dinner ends with a bowl of ice cream, but if fighters are joining us, Uncle Mike won't let them eat it because he says that ice cream and beer get men out of shape. But he eats ice cream when they're not around. And I don't mean a cup of it. Sometimes he'll eat an entire pint. With walnuts and chocolate syrup on top and everything. I kid you not. He's really something sometimes. He really is.

Aunt Karen walks with a limp because of a car accident when her sons were in college. Uncle Mike had four years left in the military before he could retire, but he took it early to take care of her. That meant losing a lot of his pension. The only reason he didn't lose all of it was because his superiors respected him enough to pull a few strings to make sure he was taken care of.

Aunt Karen can walk and get around, but with two hip surgeries and no cartilage in one of her knees, it's hard for her. Uncle Mike's a good example to me in the way he treats her. They tease each other in the kitchen, she giggles and pops his butt with her hand, and they peck kiss. He opens doors for her, helps her up the stairs, and does gentleman stuff like that.

I know he prepares hot baths for her when she comes down with headaches. And he cooks a lot of the meals, too. I asked him why they never fight, and he said they do, but they always do it in private.

Being with them has been the closest thing I've ever had to a stable family other than Grandmother. She died a few years back when she had a heart attack in the Piggly Wiggly. I was fourteen.

At Uncle Mike and Aunt Karen's I like to go for long walks outside town. They have some old bicycles from when their sons lived at home. On some days, I'd ride, and I still do, about fifteen minutes to the countryside where a pasture spreads as far as I can see. A red barn sits on the far right side of the distant hill.

On those hills above the pasture, I sometimes sit and watch the sun go down. At night the crickets, tree frogs, and locusts tweet and sing songs you can hear through closed windows. In the spring and summer, lightning bugs flash and dip in the sky, and coyotes yip-yap in the woods far away.

Thoreau said nature always gives back more than it takes. I think nature has helped keep me sane. He said the birth, life, and death cycles of nature can remind us that nothing is forever and can help us keep life in a proper perspective.

I guess so. I know the stars remind me of how small I am. And I guess I'm with everyone else in wondering where or how we got here. I learned about God at Grandmother's church, but I didn't believe everything they said. I do believe in "intelligent design," I just don't know the ID's name. I don't know the ID's ID!

Anyway, when I found that pasture a few years ago, I knew I'd never forget it. I've promised myself for a long while that one day, if I live to be an old man, I'll buy that pasture and build a house on the top of the hill with a wrap-around porch, and I'll keep some horses in that red barn. And I'll find a pretty girl and marry her. We'll sit on our back porch every evening, drink sweet tea, and watch the sun go down, and live the rest of our lives in peace. That'd be great. It really would.

Goodnight,
BB

November 7, 1998
I finished Thoreau's *Walden* and I liked it. Thoreau does a good job describing the country-side. My teacher said it's called "imagery" where he describes pictures and smells and sounds, and it makes us feel like we're right there with him. I hope I can write like that one day.

I let Uncle Mike read a little bit of my journal, and he said he could tell I was becoming a better writer. Practice makes perfect. That made me feel real good, because other than MMA, I'm not really good at anything except getting into trouble.

I'm still doing well in health and English, the stuff that deals with reading and writing, but I'm terrible at science and math. Science is kind of interesting, but I can't wrap my head around that math stuff. I complain to Uncle Mike about it and he admitted that after graduation, if you're not an architect or an engineer or something, you'll never really use anything outside addition, subtraction, division, and multiplication. And even then you'll use a calculator.

So why don't we just take a class on how to master the calculator? That'd make things a lot easier on everyone. Man, I bet it wouldn't take two weeks to teach that class. All that really makes me mad because the teachers make math sound so important. But Uncle Mike said part of growing up is doing things you don't want to do, because doing things well that you don't enjoy doing prepares you for future success.

Wait, none of that can make me mad. I choose to be mad. I gotta remind myself of that stuff.

Uncle Mike has been letting me borrow his truck on the weekends if I need it. I've taken out a girl or two who finds bad boys attractive, but it's not that much fun if you don't know them well. Besides, when they realize I'm not a bad boy, that I just look like one, and they heard all those stories about me beating up Jake, they don't stick around long.

One of them asked me if she could have my thingmajig, but she said it in front of her friends at one of those football games. She used the d-word, but I can't write that because Uncle Mike said I shouldn't use profanity. Anyway, I think the girl was just showing off. I mean, what girl says that anyway? Just blurts it out like that in front of everyone? People can be weird sometimes. They really can.

Anyway, Uncle Mike said that's how you get to know girls, by dating them. But I think dating's overrated. I'd much rather meet someone and become good friends with her, and then see if she wants to take it further. I've wondered if something is wrong with me, to not want to date, and to not be turned on by that girl when she said she wanted my thingmajig. Jake would be turned on by it. As a matter of fact, he'd make it with her and then tell everyone in school about it. That's the kind of guy he is.

The girl, she wasn't ugly, either. She was kind of cute. She came from a broken home like me, but I bet it wasn't as messed up as mine. Anyway, I was feeling a bit lonely, and Uncle Mike was always on me about not dating anyone, so I took her out. And she never tried to have sex with me when we sat in the truck at the frosty bar. We just ate a burger and a frosty and talked about how boring her classes and friends were. Well, she talked, and I listened.

Her name was Sally Jo. No kidding. Like something out of those old country black and white TV shows. Come here, Sally Jo! Over there, Mamie Jo! Don't get that chicken doodoo on your dress, Willie Jo!

Back in middle school, I kissed a few girls and even messed around with some. Just on top of the clothes stuff. But it only created drama, so I stopped. I mean, they'd stare at you all the time in the halls at school, with a smile on their face, and want to hold your hand all the time, and want you beside them, even though they never talked to you. They only talked to their friends and just wanted to have you there. All that stuff's boring to me.

The last thing I need to do is just go with it, have sex with them, and get them pregnant. And spending time and money on dates, just to see if I might want to be their boyfriend, doesn't make much sense to me. I mean, in my mind, time is actually worth more than money, and money is worth a whole lot when you're working for it.

But I think I'd love being married, if I found the right woman. We'd have sex everyday. I mean, we'd just walk around the house naked. All the time. And we'd talk and laugh and do stuff together. And we'd really talk to each other, and not to other people while wishing we could talk to each other. Man, I think it'd be a blast. I really do.

BB

May 5, 1999

School's almost over! And next week, we're going to New York City for the MMA expo. Every year, amateurs and professional fighters meet up in New York for conferences and dojo exhibitions, and young fighters get to meet national and world champions.

Uncle Mike goes every year and takes some of his fighters with him. It's expensive, but I've been saving all I can to go without tapping into my savings account. Uncle Mike goes to see old friends and keep up with the latest technology, what's selling, what new gyms are offering, all that.

It'll be my first weekend off from the dojo since I was thirteen. Tony's going, too, and about eight or nine other fighters. I've never been out of Alabama, not even Tuscaloosa County, really. I can't wait to see what's out there. I've seen New York in movies and on TV, so I'm really excited.

Goodnight!

BB

• • •

May 15, 1999

We're on the plane home from New York and I'm really glad I have a few hours to write, because man, do I have a story to tell! I met a girl! Her name's Shannon, and she's amazing! I can't stop thinking about her.

This is going to be a really long entry, because I want to write all the details just as they happened. I don't ever want to forget this one.

Outside the Hard Rock Café on our first night in NYC, after dinner with Uncle Mike and the fighters, a million people and a hundred horns blew across the streets. And she was there. I even caught her looking at me.

This blonde-haired girl with her hair pinned into a French bun. I know it's called a French bun because she told me later when I asked her about it. I thought it was really beautiful, and I wanted to know its name.

She wore a white polo shirt and khaki shorts and leather sandals. She's got the legs of a gymnast and I think that's really hot. She has these almond-brown eyes and she looked away when I caught her looking at me. But she smiled anyway, and I knew she knew I caught her. That smile of hers, with the dimples in her cheeks, just wow. I mean, wow.

Her watching me surprised me because I'm not

that impressive to look at. My shaved head isn't attractive to many girls, but I'm often complimented on my blue eyes. They turn gray when I wear black and gray, but they turn electric blue when I wear navy blue. They might could catch some real women. Like tractor beams or something. Anyway, all I wore that day was my solid black t-shirt and faded jeans. So I don't see why she liked that, either.

Shannon LaFarre, I learned her name later, carried a leather backpack and gripped the shoulder bands with her hands. I waited for her to look my way again. And when she did, I smiled the most confident smile I could come up with, and I waved at her. She leaned her head back and laughed, and that made me feel real good.

A friend tapped her shoulder and pointed up the street in our direction, and so they headed our way. I turned to James, one of my roommates. He's humble and plump. I don't think there's a bit of muscle on his legs, because he just comes to the gym for bicep curls and to walk on the treadmill.

People like James find expos real interesting, so that's why they come. He wears braces at nineteen years old, and he never goes into public without his hair gelled, even when he comes to the gym.

James asked if he knew what our plans were for the night, so I let him distract me until I could feel Shannon's group getting closer. She about passed behind me, but I took a small step back and cut her off. She almost bumped into me. She stood still a second or two, wondering if I was going to introduce myself.

So, to be playful, I just smiled and waved again. I didn't even say a single word. And she laughed, but harder this time, and it's a laugh I'll love forever. And I mean it. I'll love it forever.

I didn't believe I'd ever see her again, but later that night, we were meeting in the lobby of the hotel to visit the Empire State Building, and there Shannon was, standing near the door. I kid you not. We were staying in the same hotel. I mean, how does stuff like that happen?

Anyway, her mom, with the same hair color and eyes, was talking to her. Mrs. LaFarre was tired, but she was smiling. When Shannon looked over her shoulder and our eyes met, she smiled a soft smile at me, and I realized she already knew I was there. The look on my face must have been funny because she chuckled. But I could only stare. She was so pretty! I couldn't believe it. I mean, that was really her, and she was really standing there.

So I took a step toward her and motioned her to meet me halfway. She kept her eyes locked on mine, but she crossed her arms, probably wondering what kind of person I was, and if I could be trusted. I understand that. She's a real smart girl. Smart girls make you earn their trust.

She met me halfway, and we shook hands, and I said, "I'm Brian."

"I'm Shannon. Are you a tour group?"

"Nah. We're here for a sports expo." I didn't want to say MMA, because people think it's violent and has a bunch of meatheads.

"Oh, cool," she said.

"Where are you from?"

"Nor Cal."

"Nor Cal?" I'd never heard of such a place. Where was that, Canada?

"Northern California. My younger sister is here with her high school. They're singing in Carnegie Hall."

"When are they performing?"

"Tomorrow night."

"We'll be back by eight," I said. "When does her group go on?"

"Eight."

"I thought everybody singing in Carnegie Hall was opera singers or something."

"I thought everyone singing was high schoolers," she said, chuckling and slapping her hips with her hands. Then she slid her hands into her pockets, and I knew she was beginning to feel more comfortable with me. That made me feel good, too.

"So you're here to see your sister. And that's your mom?" I asked. Mrs. LaFarre was watching us and smiling.

"Yep," Shannon said. "But I'm also looking around. I thought about moving out here for acting, but I think I'll just stay where I am."

"Where's that?"

"L.A.—Los Angeles. So Cal. I'm moving out of West Hollywood soon. I'm going to Santa Monica."

I don't know where any of those places are, but I nodded anyway. "Oh, that's cool. Have you found a place to live yet?" I asked her.

"Ehh," she said. "Everything's so expensive. Just a studio apartment is $600 a month." (Here's a note I'll need later. Minimum wage is $5.15 right now. After taxes, $600 is equal to about 166 hours of work.)

"So, you're finished with college?" I said.

"I am. Just graduated."

"From where?"

"Pepperdine. I'm in grad school, now, for my MFA."

"MFA?"

"Yeah. Master of Fine Arts. It's a terminal degree. I can teach college if I want to. In Acting."

"Where's Pepperdine?"

"Malibu. I've been waitressing, saving money. What about you? What's your story?"

I saw a brochure for Pepperdine in the guidance counselor's office at TCHS a few years back. Peach buildings with pink, clay shingled roofs, built in what they called "Mediterranean Architecture," standing on a grassy hill, overlooking an electric-blue ocean. I'm sure that blue was doctored in Photoshop or something. I've never seen water so blue. I wondered who got to attend a school like that. Probably the really smart kids. Or the rich ones. Shannon was now officially intimidating, but I tried to recover fast.

"I'm-a, I'm-a-nineteen," I replied, tripping over my words. That wasn't truc. I'm about to be nineteen. She had me hesitating and stuttering, like a blabbering moron. But she didn't seem to notice. "I'm starting college next year. Helping my uncle right now, at his gym." That's more of a hope than a truth, but I was trying to impress her.

"Neat," she said. "What kind of gym?"

"Uh, we train MMA fighters. Mixed martial arts." I scratched the back of my head, because I was afraid of how that would go over. Shannon pulled her head back and looked at me with these real wide eyes. I was anticipating that, though, so I said, "It's all right—we're not violent. We teach dieting, core-strength, cardio. We train women there too, because we can get them in shape real fast."

"Oh, well, that sounds really interesting," she said. "I did aerobics in college, and I still go to the gym and watch what I eat. Maybe you can give me some tips."

"Sure." A second or two passed. "So where are you guys headed tonight?"

"To a Broadway play. You?"

"The Empire State Building."

"Oh, awesome! We were there last night. It's beautiful. You'll love it."

"So, you want to meet me back here at the lobby, later tonight?" I asked.

"Yeah," she said, smiling and clasping her hands together below her chin.

"It's six now. Do you think you'll be back by ten o'clock?"

"Oh, sure. I'm with my mom, so she's not going to stay out late."

I have no idea where all that confidence came from, but it was there inside me. I hadn't really liked a girl enough to talk to her in a long time. I can't even remember when the last time was. Maybe three years? I know that sounds bad, but I mean, even if I did find someone, who in the world would want to date me? With me and my history? Nobody wants to date a boy from a trailer park, unless they're from a trailer park, too.

Shannon's group started to leave, and she peeked over her shoulder at me, one last time, and smiled goodbye.

When we arrived back at the hotel a few hours later, I asked the doorman if he had seen the group from Northern California, and he said no. We were the first that had left and came back, he said. It was 10:30 p.m. or so and I wondered if I would ever see Shannon again. The thought of not seeing her worried me.

Just then, a group of students poured through

the front door. "How are you this evening?" the doorman asked, nodding his head and smiling. I got out of the way, and then Shannon stepped out from the back and walked straight toward me. My heart bounced in the bottom of my throat, just below my Adam's apple. It was the happiest I've felt in a long time.

"Hi," Shannon said, with her eyes locked on mine again. I wished I had packed my navy blue pea coat or something. I have one that Uncle Mike gave me for Christmas. That would have really set my eyes off for her, but I didn't think I'd meet a girl. Shannon's mom passed by, nodded hello at me, and waited for Shannon at the elevators.

"Did you guys have a good time?" I asked.

"Oh," she answered, touching her heart. "Fabulous. If it's okay, I'm going to change clothes and put my purse down."

After she left, I asked the doorman where we should go, and he said to walk around Times Square, watch the street performers, and make sure we tried a hot dog before we left.

Shannon returned with a skip in her step, and that made me feel real good. I mean, she was skipping because she was going to get to spend time with me! Man, I never saw that coming. She wore a grape purple t-shirt that brought out her brown eyes. And I loved that. She has some gorgeous eyes. She really does.

We walked side by side through the bustling

streets of Times Square. Locals wear a lot of black and also sunglasses, even at night. I always hear, "If you want to know where the East will be in five years, look at where the West is now." But New Yorkers are different. They walk to the beat of their own drum.

During the daytime, the city mostly smells like exhaust. Tops of skyscrapers disappear into clouds. Flashing advertisements cover the walls on most buildings. Horns constantly blow. Beeps echo as trucks shift into reverse. Car and truck tires pop over the steel sewer lids. Yells, both friendly and angry, come from all directions. "The city that never sleeps" was more real than I thought.

But at night, New York City feels like a magical world. It was everything I've seen on TV and more. Store and building lights make the city glow like a Christmas tree. And for some reason, people seem more cheerful at night. I wonder why that is. Maybe it's because they're off work and get to spend time with their friends, like I was spending with Shannon.

Street performers break-danced on mats to homemade thump and bump music, and they spun on their heads while wearing motorcycle helmets. Chinese masseuses offered Shannon and me back and neck massages. They even had recliners set up on the sidewalks and strangers were lying down on them, getting their shoulders and necks rubbed. No kidding.

"Imakeyougooddeal," the Chinese masseuses said, running their words together real fast. "Fivedolla!" By their tone, I wasn't sure if that's how they talked or if they were angry. But they smiled and waved us over, and since we were in public, I guessed they were safe. But we didn't get a massage.

Shannon wanted coffee from a place called Starbucks. She said it's growing in popularity. But we never found one open. I didn't care, though. I was having a fine time with her just walking and talking.

I asked her about her home and she brought her hands together and clapped them, like an excited kid. Everything was so fresh and new to her. I love that. She said her dad and brother grew corn and made a good living doing it, and that her mom was a stay-at-home mom. And when she asked about mine, I lied and said my dad was away on business a lot in sales and my mom was also a housewife.

"You didn't want to farm corn?" I asked, to get the conversation off me.

"No," Shannon said. She wrinkled her nose when she said it, and I thought that was real cute.

"You wanted to be an actress," I said.

"Yeah. I studied theater in college because I knew that's what I wanted to do."

"You didn't know a soul when you moved there?"

"My agent's there."

"That's amazing, Shannon," I said. "It really is."

"Aw," she answered. "That's what it takes if you want to succeed."

"But that's what I mean. Most people don't take those risks. Going after your dreams. I think that's really cool."

"Thanks," she said.

Shannon's the coolest and most laid-back girl I've ever met. I've met pretty girls before, but they're not like Shannon. She's educated, has common sense, she's smarter than me. I know that. She's driven, confident, courageous to chase her dreams, and she's older. I love that, too. When a girl is a few years older than a guy and knows how to speak to him and treat him, I've never met any guy who didn't want that over a dumb, younger girl. If the guys do, they're idiots.

Shannon didn't hide her thoughts from me. And she didn't try to impress me, either. She wasn't interested in any of my accomplishments, though there aren't many except that some of the fighters I trained won some competitions. She was just glad to have that walk with me, to be in my company. And that made me feel real happy.

There were quiet times between us, like that time we went into the CD shop and separated for a while, skimming through CDs on shoulder-tall racks. But we always knew where each other was in the room. I thought that was really cool.

Sometimes, I would look over at her, and it was like I was watching a story take place through someone else's eyes. This can't be real, I thought. Meeting a girl like her was the last thing I expected.

When it grew late, I rode the elevator with her to her floor. She was staying with her mom only a few floors above mine. She invited me to her sister's concert the next night, at 8:00 p.m., saying she had an extra ticket for me if I wanted to go. So we agreed to meet back up at Carnegie Hall the next night. I'd take a taxi.

I hadn't held Shannon's hand or tried to hug her. So when the elevator opened, I just cupped her hand in mine and gave it a gentle squeeze. Shannon smiled at me and her cheeks went pink. And she stepped off the elevator and kept smiling at me until the door closed between us.

The next morning, Uncle Mike left our group for a while to meet old friends for breakfast. And since there weren't any events at the expo we wanted to go to, two of the fighters and I went for breakfast at a café outside Manhattan.

Man, that was a great morning. Fresh flowers stood in glass vases on our table, and the morning air was clean. All felt right and in place. Birds sang in the trees (I think they're called Green Ash trees) that lined new sidewalks. We ate on a "terrace" or something like that, and the sunlight through the trees created this real beautiful shimmering effect.

"So you met a girl?" Aaron, our other room-mate, asked after the waitress brought us waters. Aaron and James had seen me with Shannon in the lobby.

"Uh-oh," James said, his mouth open all wide. I thought about stuffing it with those flowers in the vase. I didn't want those two making a big deal. They could ruin it with Shannon if they got involved. Aaron, not James, he can be real selfish and unpredictable.

"Yeah," was all I said.

Aaron is tall, lanky, with fiery red hair and a light-skinned face. He gels his hair up at the front like those beefcakes on Grandmother's old soap operas. And when he's talking to a pretty girl, he slides his right knuckles over the hair above his right ear, pretending to be shy and sweet. Man, he gets on my nerves. He really does. He always pretends to be shy around girls because that's what he thinks attracts them.

He came to the dojo only to run on the tread-mills to stay toned. I mean, when he did lift some of the dumbbells, he lifted less than James. We didn't mind, because Aaron paid, but I think he liked to tell people he trained at Mike's Dojo. And he likes trips like these to NYC because it gives him stories to tell everyone when he goes back home. He's our comic relief when he's not around. The fighters and I make fun of him all the time. I know that's bad, but it's the way it is.

Aaron took some road trips out to North and South Carolina that he talks about all the time. He's into all the arts, singing, acting. He likes to swing dance. The girls love him for that, and he knows it. Aaron also takes a golden lab puppy with him everywhere he goes, because they're "chick magnets," he says. And when the puppy grows too big and isn't cute anymore, he'll pay a fee and trade it in for a younger one. "Not every girl likes a kitten, but no girl can turn down a puppy," he told me once, while he was running on the treadmill. And he said it real slow, and with a smile that told me he had spent some time coming up with the perfect quote to describe why he did that with those puppies.

But I do have to hand it to him. I've seen those puppies work. Girls will gather around him to pet the puppy. And one thing I've noticed about him is, when he puts his mind to something, he won't stop until he gets it.

Aaron worked as a background extra on the TV show *Dawson's Creek*. During spring break at Shelton State, he made the nine-hour drive to Wilmington and asked around town where the show was filmed. After getting directions to the head office, he walked in, signed up as an extra, and just like that, he got on the show. It's amazing what we can do when we just show up.

"Will we meet her?" James asked.

"Sure," I said. But I knew I wouldn't let Aaron.

"What time's the expo?" I asked, changing the subject.

"Two p.m.," James said.

There was a fight scheduled between these two eighteen-year-olds. They're rising star fighters, but I've never heard of them. Sometimes the fighters for the expo fights are chosen for political reasons and then marketed as "an up-and-coming kid to watch." Maybe someone owed a trainer or a dojo a favor or something. It happens a lot.

Later that day while we were at the expo, I met this kid named Ian. He was twenty-two with red-brown hair and freckles, and he was a senior at Pepperdine. That's where Shannon goes to grad school. I asked him if he knew her, but he didn't.

Ian was from Ireland and his brother was selling boxing gloves at one of the booths. When our group was walking by, I heard his accent and I asked where he was from. It's the first time I'd ever talked to someone from another country. He said he was attending Pepperdine on the Os Guinness Scholarship. He said that since he was from Ireland and wanted to study theology, he got to go to school there for free. No kidding.

Later that night, I took a taxi to Carnegie Hall. There, the men were dressed in suits and tuxedos and the women wore evening gowns. Shannon warned me about that. Luckily, I had packed a black suit for the main expo event, which was a sparring match between those two "up-and-comings" I'd never heard of before.

Shannon was waiting for me with my ticket at the front door of Carnegie Hall. A huge smile was on her face when she saw me. That made me feel real good. She wore a long sleeveless black dress that covered her shoulders and stretched all the way down to her ankles. A small oval opening was cut at the top of her breasts. Wow. I had to look away because I was starting to get aroused right there in Carnegie Hall. Man, that would have been embarrassing, being aroused and stepping over people's feet and knees to get to my seat.

Shannon's earrings were a silver string with small diamonds frozen in motion while sliding down. That's the best way I can describe it, and it's still not good enough. A matching silver necklace was shaped like a V, and it lay around her neck.

She was gorgeous. Wow. Just, wow. Even her hair was curled and her eyeliner set off her eyes in this amazing way. I can't explain it. She doesn't need to wear make-up at all, I don't think. I like her just the way she is. I could just go on and on. I really could.

"Hello," she said, taking my hands in hers. She kissed my cheek and her vanilla perfume filled my nose. It came from her hair, though. I think it was her shampoo. But man, did she smell good.

When we entered the hall, maroon carpets covered shiny wooden floors and marble staircases. I was afraid to fall down them. I'd bust my knee plum open. Not that I was afraid of getting hurt, but I'd feel sorry for bleeding on that ancient carpet. I don't want to know how much it'd cost to clean it.

The auditorium seating sloped toward the stage, and the carnation-red velvet seats swung up and down, like they do at the movie theaters.

Marble balconies for the wealthy folks lined the walls with matching velvet curtains pulled back and tied by gold colored ropes. I doubt they were made out of real gold.

Shannon said, "Look at the Goth, the romance, just the class." I thought that too, but I wasn't exactly sure what all those words meant. And I wouldn't have said it like that. But being there was like stepping back into the eighteenth century or something.

Shannon and her mom had saved a seat for me, and so she led me down the center aisle to their row. Mrs. LaFarre shook my hand. Shannon and I didn't say much after that. During the concert, I wanted to hold her hand, but I decided against it. I knew it was important not to rush things.

I read in this book once that rushing romance, with a woman, is like pushing a rose to bloom before its time. If you're patient and let nature take its course, the full beauty will unfold and make all the waiting worthwhile. That's how I remember it, anyhow.

Shannon's sister's school performed on stage, and this giant orchestra sat and played below them in a pit. I'd never seen anything like it in rcal lifc. And I wished I understood Latin because I've never heard words and sounds so beautiful. I read in the program that Gabriel Faure had composed "Requiem," which is what we were listening to, after his wife died.

You can feel his sadness in the music. Anger and sadness, yet, at other times, a deep, peaceful acceptance. It had these nice, soothing sounds in certain parts, and at other times it was like being in a haunted house or something. Man, was it depressing. And I hoped the depressing parts would end soon. Because I wanted to be happy, especially with Shannon there.

After the show, Shannon and I took a taxi to a docked ship, which was an after-party for all the choruses. There, we joined her mom and their group. Their travel package included a tour around the Statue of Liberty. So I got to ride on a boat for the very first time! And it was really cool. It was a double-decker! It wasn't big enough to be a cruise ship, but it was larger than a fishing boat, if that makes sense.

Once we got on the ship and left the docks, the city lights, the noise, and the crowds just died out. Like turning the volume down on a radio. And from the sea, as the boat skipped across the waves, New York City's lights left a thousand colorful, shimmering trails on the rocking waters. That sounded like Thoreau!

Upstairs on the boat, there was a restaurant with a balcony that overlooked the bar. Downstairs was a wooden dance pad for people to get their groove on. During dinner, Shannon and I sat with her mom, sister, and some of the students. Shannon and I couldn't keep our eyes off each other. When she smiled at me, all was right again. It was like I had been preparing for that night with her all my life. I didn't want it to end!

The bartenders weren't checking IDs, so all the high school kids from Nor Cal were getting hammered. I wasn't against having a whiskey or two, but I could already hear Uncle Mike yelling at me about staying in shape.

It was hardly a time for Shannon and me to talk. It was too loud. The students at our table were yelling above the noise and talking about the wine. "It has hints of chocolate and tannins," like they were a bunch of connoisseurs or something. Then, one of the teachers, Dr. Sutter, apologized to us, but she talked with a slur. "I'm thorry, but the winesth free."

One of the teachers at our table wore a toupee. Dr. Sutter kept pointing it out to everyone. Since they were friends, he didn't seem to mind, or maybe he was just pretending. One of the students leaned over and whispered to me, "I knew about that toupee the entire time." Wow, I thought. What a bunch of geniuses.

I had enough, and that's when people started making their way to the dance floor. The teachers and Shannon's mom just sat and watched everyone. An announcer said we were approaching the Statue of Liberty. So, I used that as an excuse and invited Shannon outside on the balcony. "Yeah!" Shannon said, her face lighting up.

Shannon's mom propped her chin on top of her hand and looked up at me through her eyelashes, smiling. Shannon had stood without thinking, then looked back at her mom real quick. "Is that okay?"

Mrs. LaFarre nodded and said, "You kids have fun."

Shannon slid her hand through the loop of my arm and I led her out the door. The wind hit us as soon as we stepped outside, so I took off my coat and hung it over her shoulders. She adjusted it, thanked me, and we walked to the railing where we could watch the city lights.

I stood behind her and she leaned against my chest. The salty air from the sea filled our noses, and I could hear the front of the boat bursting through the bumps in the water. The way we stood, the boat rocked left and right, left and right, but it was gentle and we didn't have to hold onto anything.

I caressed the back of her arm, near her elbow, my way of asking permission to touch her. She rested the back of her head on my shoulder, and I could smell the vanilla in her hair again. I love that smell. She took in the city, while I took in her. I've never had feelings for anyone before. I know I could say yes to her. I could say yes to anything she wants or needs. I know that all she has to do is tell me what she wants in life, her hopes and dreams, and I'll do everything to give them to her.

When I experienced all that with her, I knew it was real. Someone said this once. When you fall in love, no one can tell you you're in love. You just know. Others will even make fun of you for falling so soon, but it's just because they don't understand. I get that now.

Falling in love is really beautiful and terrifying all at once. The feeling is real strong and con- trolling. I can see why it directs people's decisions and emotions. And then there's that terrifying reality that it can all come crashing down at any second. Love is dangerous. But it's beautiful. And I knew then, right there, holding her in my arms as the city floated by, that I would do everything in my power to be with her, no matter how many months or years might pass.

I know one thing. From now on, when I see people in love, I'll be happy for them, no matter their age. Because now, I know what it's like.

The Statue of Liberty was gray in the distance, but up close, it's an olive green. And it's gigantic! It was built by a man from France in the 1880s, as a gift to the Americans for their independence from the British. The funding to build it came from donations across the USA. I read once that a group of children sent in their money instead of going to a circus, homeless men took up a collection at a local bar, and a kindergarten class from Iowa sent in one dollar and three cents.

It's amazing how you remember stuff like that and forget everything else. Like, I can't remember what the bones in my ankles are called, and I had to memorize that stuff for exams last year. But I remember facts from history I read years ago. I guess, sometimes, we just remember what we want to remember.

"What are you thinking about?" she asked me. I was almost too embarrassed to tell her. Stuff from high school history? That would sure flatter her, wouldn't it. I just shook my head.

"Nothing," I said.

"I like that I can be quiet with you," she said. "And I was thinking about how that statue makes me realize how limited our time is. And how our words and actions create ripples in the world. The people who built it, did they have any idea the impact it would have on future societies?"

Man, I love the way she talks.

"I don't know," I whispered. I wonder if she had

63

any idea the impact she already had on me. "Life doesn't last long, does it?" I asked her.

"No, I don't think so. I'm learning that more as I get older."

"I'm glad you get to chase your dreams," I said.

"You sound like you believe that's not possible for you," she replied. "Do you believe you can do anything you set your mind to?" she asked, turning her face to me.

I don't know what's possible and what isn't, anymore. But her example's awesome. "I believe I can try," I said. "But things are different in Alabama."

"People are people, no matter where they live, Brian," she said.

I know I don't need to make any excuses anymore. Some people's situations don't allow them to chase every dream that comes around. Some people are too busy wondering where their next paycheck is coming from. But I didn't say anything. I appreciated her spirit, and left it at that. She inspires me, and I like that.

Once the boat passed the statue, it went straight back to the dock. When I opened the sliding glass door for Shannon and me to go back inside, the music had stopped, and everyone talked in drunk language. Mrs. LaFarre was gathering her coat and purse and said a van would be driving their group back to the hotel. I didn't think there was enough room for me.

I felt that Shannon needed to ride back with her people. I don't know why. I just knew instinctively. And she didn't ask to join me in my taxi ride back. I didn't want to push things, and I had kept her from her mom for some time.

"Do you have plans later tonight?" I asked Shannon. And when she shook her head, I asked, "You want to meet me in the lobby again?"

"Sure," she said, with a nod and a smile. "I'll change clothes, and I'll meet you there."

Back in my room, I may have set a world record for how fast a man can change his clothes. Aaron was getting ready for another walk around New York with some of the others. But James was already in his boxers and in bed, watching TV.

I slipped on my black hooded dojo sweatshirt and sweatpants, which Uncle Mike gave me after one of the fighters I helped train won Regionals. The dojo logo is stitched over the heart and reads "Mike's Dojo" with a curve in the *j* forming a man's elbow, and a boxing glove over the fist. I've only worn it a few times, because I don't want to ruin it. I'm proud of those sweats.

I knew Shannon would take awhile, so I grabbed my journal and headed downstairs. The hotel restaurant was closed, but the doorman said I could sit at one of the tables, as long as I didn't disturb the teepee napkins and the perfectly placed silverware.

I went ahead and started jotting down bullet

points about this trip, so I could hang onto the details. This will be a story to remember. I just know it will. So, I wrote about Shannon, about how beautiful she looked, how wonderful of a person I think she is, and how all these new feelings I never knew existed have overtaken me.

I feel so excited and alive, because of her. And I still feel those same feelings, just as strong, as I'm writing this. But it hurts being away from her, and it's only been a day since we met. I hope it doesn't always feel like this, while we're away from each other.

Fifteen long minutes went by, and as soon as I was lost in writing parts of our story, I heard her say hello.

"Hi," I answered, and my pencil scratched a big mark across the page. She startled me! That was embarrassing, and she noticed and laughed.

"Whatcha doing?" she asked, as her eyes swept over my writings.

I said that I wrote in my journal so that when I become an old man and my memory fades, I'll have the stories to read. It's also great practice, if you want to be great at writing. I can already tell a difference in the way I write now, versus when I first started my journal.

"Am I in it?" she asked, with a grin.

"I was just getting to that," I said. I was using tones in my voice I had never used before. I was gentle and caring and genuine. Those are the best words I can think of. I stood and kept my eyes locked on hers. Our cheeks touched as I kissed her temple. "But it would be dumb to write about a woman when I could be spending time with her." That sounded really eloquent coming out, and I was proud of myself for that.

"Good idea," she replied, clucking her tongue. "And very poetic."

I ushered her to a couch in a quiet corner that overlooked the lobby and all the people coming and going from Times Square. People of all colors and shapes and sizes, and speaking all these different languages. It was amazing to watch.

"So, you want to be an actress," I said, when we got still and quiet. The cushions sank real deep when we sat in them. I wanted to know everything about her. Shannon's heart, her mind, her views on the entire world. I reached out and touched her hand as it lay between us. She caressed mine, too, and that felt really good.

"I do," she said, smiling at me.

"Do you think you'll ever be famous?" I asked.

"Maybe!" she said, rising up. "The money would be nice!" We laughed. Man, she's great.

"What else do you want?" I went on.

"I want to sing," she said, searching my face for some kind of approval.

"You sing?"

"I've been singing since I was a kid."

"I sing, sometimes," I said.

"Really?"

"Yeah. In the shower." That wasn't true. But I wanted to hear her laugh, and it worked. Man, I love her laugh. "What else?" I said, before we could get distracted by something else.

"I want to be married one day," she said, just matter-of-fact. "And I want my husband and me to be that couple whose friends know they can come to our house and feel at home. I want to throw wine and dinner parties."

"Be popular?"

"No," she said, real quick. "Just do nice things for friends. Like that old proverb, to have friends, be friendly."

"What about Nor Cal? You won't miss your family and friends?"

"Sure I will. But there are holidays and summers. What about you? What do you want?"

Ever since I got in trouble with the law, I just assumed I'd always be working at the dojo. But when she asked me that question, I knew I wanted more than that. For the first time in my life, I didn't want to stay at the dojo. I wanted to go and do and see things that would wow me. I wanted to meet people like Shannon, and be as different from me as she is. I never realized I wanted any of that until I came to NYC, and until I met her.

"Here's a trick," she said. "If you had an unlimited amount of money, and no one's opinion of you mattered, and you could do anything you wanted, anything in the entire world, what would you do? One of my professors said if you can answer that question, that's what you're supposed to do with your life."

"I'd study psychology and open my own business," I answered. I was surprised I said that. Then I said, "Find out why people do the things they do." Earlier this year, I heard that licensed psychologists in South Carolina made $160.00 an hour. That's how things go now that it's 1999.

"You mean a clinic?"

"Yeah."

"What would you do at the clinic?" she asked.

"Help people, listen to their problems, tell them what to do."

She laughed. "Just tell them what to do, huh?" She thought I was joking, but I wasn't. That's what I wanted to do. Sure, I know it's not that easy, and I'm not always right, but when I was put on the spot for the first time, that was my answer.

"Well," I said, trying to recover real quick. "I'd find out where they needed help, and I'd make sure they got it."

"Like a therapist?"

"Yeah." That was the term I was looking for. "I've always been interested in understanding why people do what they do."

"So you want to help people," she said, and she held my hand between hers, like a sandwich. She closed her eyes and rested her head on the couch. I could tell my hopes and dreams meant something nice to her, and that made me happy.

"What is it?" I asked, lowering my voice, trying to sound sexy, and inching closer to her.

"I can't believe this is happening," she whispered.

"What?" I knew exactly what she was saying, but I wanted to hear it from her.

"Meeting you in New York. A boy from Aaalabaaama," she said, spreading the syllables out. Her laugh turned into a yawn, and she covered it with her hand.

"Too bad you're going to L.A. and me back to Alabama," I said. "But I'm happy for you and I'm proud of you."

"For what?" she asked.

"Moving to L.A. by yourself, not knowing anyone. Going to grad school. That's cool. It's courageous."

"I don't see it that way."

"No?"

"In my mind, I wanted to do it, so I did." Man, I fell in love with her all over again, right there on that couch. A load of tourists poured into the hotel, laughing and yelling across the room. I pretended to watch them, but I was thinking about how much I wanted to be more like Shannon. What if I adopted that attitude? If you want to do something, figure out a way to do it, and just go do it. As long as you're not hurting anyone, why not?

"Do you want to go to my room for a while?" I asked. "My roommate will be there, but he'll be asleep."

"Sure," she said. She didn't bat an eye or even question my intentions. She trusted me, and that meant a lot, because where I grew up I was taught not to trust anyone.

Shannon and I held hands all the way to my room, and when we entered, the TV played *Mad About You* and sent a soft glow along the walls. The show was muted. James was lying on his side with his back turned to us, and he raised his head from his pillow. "Oh, hi there," he said, half waving.

"Hello," Shannon answered, smiling.

Then he nose-dived right back into his pillow, and fell asleep. Shannon lay on my bed beside me. I propped my head onto my hand and elbow and I gazed down at her, ready to listen to anything she wanted to tell me.

We talked about all kinds of stuff. She said that in order to know the best time for corn harvest, you pay attention to the color of the silk. She described how to water over 100 acres of corn at once, what farmers do when there's a drought, or what plan B is if the tractors and equipment fail.

I had never cared too much to see Nor Cal until I met her. And based on what she described, I imagined her home as a white two-story farmhouse with a wrap-around porch and a screen door that bangs when it shuts. I pictured her house on top of a hill, surrounded by fields of corn with golden silk tops, waving in the wind and disappearing over the horizon. The kind of place where you would want to walk and walk and never come back. Man, that sounded wonderful. It kind of reminded me of that pasture I still ride my bike to.

She busted out laughing and rubbed her eyes. "What is it?" I said.

"I hate the farm. That's why I moved to L.A. But here I am, talking about it like an excited kid. What's Alabama like?" she asked. I think she wanted to stop talking about Nor Cal.

I rolled over on my back, and then she hovered over me. We were taking turns. She rested her elbow across my chest and propped her head in her palm. A lock of her hair fell over her fingers, and I tucked it back behind her ear. Wow.

I talked only about the good times I could remember. I did know a few boys whose parents let me come over and hang out. With them, I saw what a normal family looked like. I told her those stories instead of how I really grew up. I talked about four-wheeler riding with boys who lived near that pasture I love to visit, jumping off a bluff and into a "blue hole," and swimming in the creek.

I talked about watching the tree leaves seesaw down until they landed in the water and provided rafts for ladybugs, butterflies, and dragonflies. I described the humid summers, and those summer nights on Lake Tuscaloosa where people from New England who we called the "Yankees" came for vacation and talked with sharp accents.

I spoke of fishing while being surrounded by the trees in autumn, with their yellow and red leaves, like the color of dark sugar. I talked about building campfires beside the waterfalls during wintertime while being surrounded by a white wilderness, the beauty of a red cardinal sitting on a snowy limb, and then the springtime bringing us green fields, wild daffodils, and the smell of honeysuckles in the air.

I made it all sound real good. And it worked, too. I can make myself sound real smart when I want to. I really can. "My Uncle Mike and Aunt Karen helped raise me because my parents weren't around a lot. But I know one thing. If I ever get married, I promise I'll be the best husband and father ever. I'll never yell or scream at my kids. I'll provide for them, protect them, and I'll be there for them when they need me. They'll be glad I'm their dad. And my wife will be glad I'm her husband. Because she'll know that she won't be loved better anywhere else."

Shannon leaned toward my face and brushed her nose against mine. Her smile and her eyes had desire in them, and that really turned me on. But I was scared to death of ruining it. So, we didn't have sex. My hand caressed her cheek. She closed her eyes and pushed her face deeper into my hand, not wanting an inch of her cheek to go unnoticed. She was so beautiful, so affectionate.

I leaned up and kissed her. It was our first kiss. I embraced her bottom lip with mine, pausing. I let go and pulled back. Then I kissed her chin and neck and her lips again. While at her neck, I felt her pulse against my lips. She drew a breath that kind of shook her voice, and then she let out this soft moan that sent these tremors throughout my body. I definitely had never experienced that before. It was amazing. I don't think I'll ever forget it.

After a while, Shannon laid her head over my heart and I ran my fingers through her hair. She chuckled, saying my heart was pounding. But I didn't care. She skated her fingers across my chest. And we lay like that until daybreak. Sometime later, I'm not sure how long, but she raised her head and peck kissed my lips, and pulled a yellow ribbon from her pocket. She moved to tie her hair back, and I said, "No. I like your hair down." She smiled, laid the ribbon on the end table, and laid her head back on my chest.

"Are you all right?" I asked, after she was quiet awhile.

"Yeah. Just thinking about my mom."

"About what?"

"She's been acting weird lately." Shannon sat

up. "She's irritable, and all her kids have either graduated or are about to, and she feels like she's not needed anymore." She was staring at the wall now. "You seem like you really care," she said, looking back at me.

"I do care," I said. That even hurt me a little. "What makes you think I wouldn't care?"

"I wondered if there were still caring men left in the world."

"Did something happen with the guys in college?" I asked.

"Some. A lot of lying and cheating. I hate it when people lie." Ouch. That bothered me a lot. Because I had already told some lies about the way I grew up.

"I'm sorry," was all I could say. I was sorry for both. That I lied to her, and that she had been lied to by boys she dated.

Tears built and one spilled out of her left eye and ran along the side of her nose. She wiped it off. "No, I'm sorry. For being like this," she said.

"It's all right," I said.

"I understand the importance of focusing on the good in people," she said. "Drawing that out and affirming them. Helping them see what they can't see in themselves. But it's not easy."

"Do you think people are naturally good?" I asked. I really wanted to know what she thought.

"I think people are just people," she said. "And they decide what to do." She sounded like Uncle

Mike. He'd love her. "What are you thinking about?" she asked.

I wanted to tell her that I thought she was one of the most beautiful creatures I had ever met. How could a woman her age be filled with so much insight, courage, and wisdom? "Nothing," I said. "Just listening." Then, she laid her head on my chest again, and I felt her body rise at every breath she took. I ran my fingers through her hair again, and she fell asleep right there in my arms. It was the greatest night of my life. At least, it's been the greatest night of my life so far.

I read in a book, I can't remember the author's name, but he said that many relationships fall apart because the man treats his woman as a problem to be solved, rather than a mystery to be known and loved. I really like that. If Shannon and I can be together, I never want to screw it up like those guys did.

When I walked Shannon to her room at 6 a.m., we exchanged home phone numbers and said we'd be in touch. "Thank you for listening," she said. "And for being a good guy." Those were her parting words to me, which I know I'll never forget. No one's ever told me I was a good guy. I thought I was a loser, a train wreck, and jaded because of my childhood.

I kissed her forehead, and then we made out in the hall, and that was wonderful. She's a really good kisser. Her flight left a few hours later.

Back in my hotel room, I found her yellow ribbon on the table. I smelled it and it still held the smell of her vanilla shampoo. I lay down and fell asleep with it wrapped around my fingers. I have it right here with me, as I'm writing all this. I keep smelling it and reliving my memories with her. And I just had to write it down. I want to be with Shannon forever.

A part of me wishes I could say that Shannon and I met in this real dramatic way, and I saved her life from street thugs or something. But this is what happened instead. We saw each other on a busy street, we got caught in each other's tractor beams, saw each other again in the same hotel we were both staying in, and went for a long walk and talk at night, in a city of sparkling lights.

We went to a symphony concert in Carnegie Hall and on a riverboat ride, and we saw the Statue of Liberty and held each other against the cold. We laughed and talked and she cried in my arms that night, and we exchanged lovers' kisses goodbye. If that's not romantic, I don't know what is.

A part of me also wishes I'd never met Shannon, because now I know who's out there and who's missing from my life. If I never see her again, and I have to dream about her for the rest of my life, that sounds like a sad life I don't want to live. So I'm going to have to come up with something. A plan.

When I was a boy, people warned me that your first heartbreak is the worst. They say first loves never last because we're kids. But what they don't tell you is that feeling of "inloveness" hurts even while the fire still burns hot. It's both wonderful and painful at the same time, like a two-way street. And now, given the distance between us, with her in So Cal, and me in Alabama, I feel like two souls, who were once united, have been torn apart. It's beautiful and depressing and gut-wrenching all at once.

I literally cannot stop thinking about her, and that scares me.

BB

May 16, 1999

I'm back at Uncle Mike and Aunt Karen's, and this morning, I woke up and Shannon was my first thought. She was my last thought last night, before I went to sleep. The sun's rays came through my window, filled the room, and warmed my face. I wonder if these feelings are what heaven will be like. I kept Shannon's ribbon on my pillow beside me. It helped me feel like she's still here with me.

I'm not sure why, but I see parts of home differently, too. I've also noticed that there are more red birds and blue birds in the neighborhood. They perch in the willow trees and swoop and chase each other across the yard. Yesterday, when I went for a walk in my favorite pasture, the Yellowhammers and Chickadees were everywhere.

Yellow swallowtail butterflies, with their charcoal striped wings, were all over the wildflowers. The woodpeckers rattled away in the trees. Two weeks ago, those sounds were annoying to me, but now, it sounds more like a song. I stopped to ask myself what was wrong with me for everything to be so awesome in the world, and then I remembered. So this is what being in love is like.

Shannon has been everywhere with me. We talk when I dress in my room, while I shave, and when I drive Uncle Mike's truck. Today, I imagined her in the passenger seat. She wore sunglasses, the wind was in her hair, and she laughed at something I said. We passed through the countryside where the Arabian horses graze on the hills at Ricky Blackwell's farm.

Shannon stuck her arm out the window and skipped it up and down like a racing dolphin. And the more I try not to think about her, the harder it is not to. I'm scared to death I'll never see her again.

I need to get some sleep.

I love Shannon LaFarre. Goodnight Shannon! Goodnight people of the world! I hope everyone has a good night's rest.

BB

• • •

May 23, 1999

Now that the weather's warmer, I've been helping Uncle Mike mow the grass again. But now I've been cutting it in plaid designs. That really impressed him. I've been helping Karen around the house more. I've skimmed through some of her cookbooks, and I've started learning how to cook and help her with some of the meals.

"What's gotten into you?" Uncle Mike asked the other morning in the kitchen. He stood with his hands on his hips and he was wearing a big grin. Aunt Karen dried plates with a towel and pressed her lips together to keep from laughing.

I had dressed the table for them. Made-from-scratch biscuits, eggs and bacon bought at Johnny's farm, juice from oranges I pushed through a juicer, and boiled blackberries to smother the biscuits. I made it all myself.

"I just want to do a good job," I said, shrugging. "I appreciate you and Aunt Karen looking after me." At the dojo, I've been more of an encourager to the fighters, saying things like, "Good form," and "That hit was solid! Good job!" I even went to the bank yesterday and asked the president about stocks and money market portfolios. I don't have the money to do it, but I want to learn.

I need a plan if Shannon and I are going to be together. And I need to be fast. I can't risk the chance of not being in her life, and her finding someone else.

I also know that the life I live will never be attractive to someone like Shannon. A woman, I've learned, needs stability and certainty that a man will be committed to his family. That way, she can build a nest and raise kids. At least, that's what Tony's uncle said the other day at the dojo. And it makes sense. I want to provide that for her. If I can become successful at something, or at least take a great step in that direction, maybe we can be together.

Uncle Mike tried talking some sense into me when I was a sophomore, but I wouldn't listen. My grades weren't the best. I had to take the ACT, and I scored a twenty. I didn't even study for it. That score's not very good, but I didn't care.

At sixteen, I was making money at the dojo. It was more than anyone my age was making, but it still wasn't much. Uncle Mike said I would never make much money in MMA and that I really needed to think about a career. "You can work hours for dollars or you can create ideas for millions," he once said. "Is this really what you want to do for the rest of your life?" he asked me last year. "Even if you say yes, you don't know, because you're too young to know. Interests change as we get older."

"Maybe I'll open my own dojo one day," I said.

"Maybe you will," he said. "And if you don't?

You won't have a college education to fall back on. Karen and I own this house and the lot. The dojo. We're debt free. I have my retirement. Karen has her insurance. You don't have those things. Besides, you don't have training in business, either. And if you opened a dojo, you'd have to do it in a major city. You need to go to college, Brian. Get a degree in business or something."

How can I go to college, though? I can't afford it, and Uncle Mike can't afford to send me. I'll never get an academic scholarship, and given my juvenile background, I'm not eligible for grants or student loans. I know I could probably go to community college next fall, go ahead and get started, but that means I'll still be separated from Shannon. And we need to be together.

Ever since I was fifteen, my goal was to stay and get a job in Tuscaloosa. I didn't believe I would live as long as I have. I thought I'd die young. The future didn't seem that bright to me, growing up. And now, after meeting Shannon, I know I don't want to spend the next ten years working in the dojo, or even owning one. I want to be with her.

Most of the men who come to the dojo are angry. Their sisters are on drugs, or they're on drugs. Their dad was abusive to them growing up, or their brother beat on them. Some of them have been in prison. Not all of them, but most of them. In Tuscaloosa, the crowd's rougher.

And that's the kind of men I see Uncle Mike

dealing with. Though I love and respect him for how he's helped them, I know now that's not what I want for the rest of my life. But I feel like I've dug myself into a hole.

BB

July 5, 1999

Last month, outside the dojo, we heard tires squealing and gun shots in the parking lot. It was a drug deal gone wrong. But it's irritated that old wound in my head that won't go away. It's time for me to get out of here. But I'm still trying to figure out how.

Two months have passed since I was with Shannon in NYC, and I still think about her everyday. I haven't called her. And I don't want to until I have a plan. I'm not sure if this decision is the best one, but I just don't know what to do.

I called an advisor at Shelton State and learned that in order to practice counseling and work as a therapist, I need a master's degree. My bachelor's could be in any field but psychology would be the best fit to prepare for grad school. After my master's, I have to conduct over 100 hours of counseling in practicum, serve under the guidance of a therapist for two years, and then I can purchase a license and open my own practice.

That would take seven to eight years, full-time. Going to school for that long seems like an eternity. Considering tuition and books, I can only afford one or two classes per semester, even if I live with Uncle Mike and Aunt Karen and go to community college. But I'd like to go to school in L.A. so I can be with Shannon.

I'll think of something.

BB

July 23, 1999

I think I'm onto something.

I remembered Ian talking about the Os Guinness Scholarship. So I looked up Pepperdine on Aunt Karen's computer. I couldn't find anything about the scholarship, so I called their admissions department.

They said if I was from Ireland, and wanted to study theology, and had a signed document from my church pastor that I would serve in the Irish church ministry after finishing my degree, the Guinness beer company will pay for my tuition. I don't have to apply through Guinness, but through Pepperdine. I don't know if they forward the documents to the Guinness company for review or not. They didn't say, and I didn't ask, because I didn't want to sound suspicious.

I made a list of the documents I need to submit with the application: a passport, a student visa, high school transcripts, and American ACT scores. On top of that, Pepperdine requires three letters of recommendation: two from high school teachers, and one from my church pastor, stating my intent to return to Ireland and serve under his pastoral guidance.

I might can convince Pepperdine that I'm Irish and go to school there for free. That way, I can be with Shannon. I know I can't afford on-campus housing, since it's $800 a month. And Pepperdine requires all freshmen to live on campus. The only way out is to tell them I have family in the area I can live with. I don't know any students in Malibu I can split rent with, and every housing post I see on the Internet is just as expensive as living on campus.

I'll have to befriend some students and live off campus and split rent. So, I've decided to try to go to Pepperdine anyway, just show up, and worst-case scenario, I stay at a hotel for a few nights until I can get to know some people. Maybe I can crash on someone's couch for a while. If I'm there, I think I can come up with a plan because I'll have a better grasp on what my options are.

I don't have to show Pepperdine my actual passport and student visa. They just want a copy of them, which show my photo, date of birth, serial numbers, etc. I think I can make some fakes. I know this is bad and it's a lot of lying, but I don't know any other way.

I'm going to push forward until I hit a brick wall.
BB

August 2, 1999

I've ordered a passport. It cost me $50.00. Everything's looking good. A lot has happened, and I'll tell you about it.

I ordered copies of my ACT scores and high school transcripts. My transcripts came in an envelope and the principal had signed his signature over a glued seal. I ordered the transcripts and ACT scores so I'd have ideas on how to create the fake ones.

I looked at pictures of Ireland's student visas on the Internet, I studied their layouts, and then I created replicas on Aunt Karen's computer. I found a high school in Galway, Ireland, on the west coast, which I used as my alma mater. When I created the Irish school envelopes and letter-heads, I copied the crest from the high school's website, and I forged their principal's signature on the documents. Just writing all this down is making me nervous.

Since Atlanta's only a three hour drive away, and that's where ACT headquarters are, I created the ACT replicas, and I plan to drive over to Atlanta to mail them to Pepperdine. Pepperdine requires that the ACT scores be mailed from ACT headquarters, so all I need to do is make sure the letter is stamped "Atlanta."

I paid James and Aaron $50.00 to pose as a

principal and church pastor and write the letters of recommendation for me. They had some of their friends help them, and I said the letters were props in a high school play my cousin was playing in.

But here was a dilemma. The high school transcripts have to be sent from Ireland. So after some prowling and researching on the Internet, I found a website called Elance where you can pay people from all over the world to complete freelance projects. So I searched the database for Irish artists and reached out to a girl and offered to pay her to mail business envelopes to a California address for me.

She doesn't know what's in them, and that doesn't matter. She's getting paid to just drop some letters in the mail for me. Who wouldn't take that gig? It's not like I wanted her to mail a heavy boxed package with oil stains and a fuse hanging out of it. Just to be light hearted, I told her they were cards for an April Fools' joke we were playing on some friends. I will mail her a manila envelope filled with additional money for postage and the sealed envelopes with the Pepperdine addresses.

All the Irish girl has to do is pay for the postage using the extra money I included, then drop them off at the local post office. The entire transaction will cost me about $30.00.

I needed to know the Irish accent. I thought

about going to Ireland and learning street names and the accent in Galway, and I even looked into doing that. After working at the dojo all these years, and after Grandmother took a cut to help raise me, all I have is about $1,800.00 in my savings. Roundtrip airfare to Dublin from Atlanta is $600.00, and even if I stay on people's couches, I'm looking at an extra $500.00 for food and travel. I just can't afford it.

So instead, I visited three libraries here in town. I read articles on Ireland in the encyclopedia, read some travel journals on the Internet about Galway and the west coast, and I rented a VHS of every single documentary about Ireland I could find. I only found two, and they were about the Irish Republican Army. But every person interviewed was Irish, and the documentaries were both over an hour long. So I was able to listen and practice the accents and I learned a lot about Irish history and culture along the way. I'd write it all down for you, but it'd take too long.

It took about a month of thinking and planning and doing my research for me to come up with all these ideas and stuff, but I wanted to tell the overall story. Anyway, that's how I'm hoping to pull all this off. It's a crazy idea, but so crazy it might work. Sometimes an action can be so bold, people just miss it. Like Aaron and those puppies and him just showing up at *Dawson's Creek*.

I can't wait to see Shannon again. I hope she'll be glad to see me!

Goodnight!

BB

Chapter 2

August 22, 1999
It's been forever since I've written, but it's because I've been so busy. I'm actually at Pepperdine now. The plan worked, and I was accepted, and I'll tell about it all real soon. I will say, it's the first week of school, and things haven't worked out like I thought they would. But I'm surviving. Uncle Mike's military books said you have a plan until you go into battle, and then that plan goes out the window.

I didn't expect all the loneliness of being out here not knowing anyone, and having to lie about who I am. And living by myself doesn't help matters, either. I'm sleeping in the university library, which stays open 24/7. It's three stories tall. I'm sitting on my sleeping bag right now with my back to my pillow and leaning against a bookcase. I'm on the third floor where periodicals and dictionaries are, and I have a battery powered lantern. The air conditioner is buzzing, and I'm surrounded by the smell of old books and walls that smell like they were painted a few weeks ago.

I'm showering and brushing my teeth in the gym, and I've been keeping my clothes in two lockers there. I had to rent them for $50.00 a semester, and I had to buy two combination locks at the CVS pharmacy in Malibu. There's a laundromat at the upperclassmen apartments, so I use that. I packed everything I could into two suitcases and flew out here. I have everything I need.

I haven't reached out to Shannon, but I plan to as soon as I find housing. If I don't, it will be impossible to hide the fact that I'm sleeping in the library. That'll be a red flag, right there. Pepperdine's student enrollment is only 3,000 so I'm making sure to eat breakfast real early in the cafeteria and then lunch and dinner real late, after all the crowds are gone. That will help make sure I don't run into her. Also, I don't have to talk to a lot of people and risk them seeing through my fake Irish accent.

I can't stick as close to my diet since I don't have my own kitchen, but I'm making do. The caf food's actually pretty good. There's baked salmon, grilled or broiled chicken, and all the fruits, salads, and vegetables you want. In California, they care more about personal health. So all the meat's always fresh.

My only real expense is food, and I ordered my books online. Every student has a mailbox on campus. And I'm trying to think of a way to make some money on the side so I don't eat up all my savings. I've put in an application to be a personal trainer at Malibu Gym. It's on the west side of town, and if I get the job, I'll have to take a bus there.

Regarding the Ireland deal, what wasn't sent through the mail from my contact in Dublin, I submitted through email to the international representative students office. I told Uncle Mike and Aunt Karen I had accepted a job at Malibu Gym with a track to earn my certification in personal training. I couldn't bear to tell the truth. I was afraid they'd try to stop me from coming here.

Personal trainers make $15.00 or so an hour, but it's thousands of dollars and countless hours to get certified, so it's not worth it to me. You can make some good money when you train people with weights, cardio, and nutrition, but you need a college degree in nutrition for anyone to take you seriously. Everything costs money.

On the lighter side, Malibu and Pepperdine are everything I imagined and more. Malibu has only 12,000 people living here because it's a retirement town. And Pacific Coast Highway, or "PCH," connects Santa Monica to Malibu and goes all the way up past San Francisco. It's the highway along the coast you see in all the movies.

The best way I can describe it is that on the left side of PCH the sun leaves a sparking white trail on crystal blue waters. On clear mornings, the ocean is electric blue. And on overcast days, it's a robin's egg blue. It just depends on the day. And to the right sits the rocky bluffs and green hills.

Malibu has a creek that's lined with trees and trimmed shrubs. Shopping outlets and a playground are squared in by boutiques, along with coffee shops, cafés, and a four-screen cinema. And down the street on the left as you come in from LAX (the airport) is a bank, a yogurt shop, Diedrich's coffee shop, Ralphs grocery store, and CVS. That's it.

Pepperdine stands on a hill overlooking the town and coast. Its front lawn is as long as a football field with a pond surrounded by reeds and "coral trees" whose gray limbs are like creepy fingers, but their tops are covered with these beautiful, fiery orange blossoms. Ducks swim there, deer eat the grass under the trees, and hummingbirds are always darting and swooping between the blooms. It's like a little slice of heaven.

On my first day, I walked around campus and checked out the dorms. Pepperdine's buildings stand on platforms, like a giant set of steps. It starts at the graduate student apartments on the tallest hill. Next step down is the law and business school. Next step after that are the upperclassmen apartments. Next step after that are the dorms, the main part of campus, and the soccer field.

After that, it's the baseball field, outdoor swimming pool, and basketball gym. And the last step is the grassy lawn of Alumni Park and a set of tennis courts. Then, there's the ocean. Everywhere on campus, you can see the ocean. It's amazing.

I wish Darren was here to see all this and experience it with me. He'd love it and I bet he'd have straight As, too. He was a smart guy.

As far as making friends goes, it's not easy for me. I've already found the freshmen to be too immature. "Have you made out with anyone? Have you pinned a girl yet? Do you have a girlfriend?" That's all I ever hear. I was over all that talk in junior high school. Then it's, "What's your name? What's your major? Where are you from? Which dorm are you staying in?"

On my first night here, the night before the first day of school, the university president had a party at his house for all the freshmen. His name is Dr. Kipling, he's really nice, and his backyard overlooks the coast and campus. The tables outside were covered with white cloths and loaded with these real delicate finger foods that I was afraid to touch, because they looked too perfect, and then there were bowls of pink punch. A catering team in black slacks and white tuxedo shirts served everyone. Like we were at some kind of rich and famous party.

A live band played classic rock on a small stage and there was a giant stop light beside them blinking on and off with the music. Red, yellow, and blue. Not green. And I met a lot of different freshmen. When they started with their questions about where I was from, I thought I'd have a bit of fun with it.

I talked in my Irish accent about growing up in Ireland, and I made up all these stories as I went along. I talked about dancing on pub tables in kilts, and fights breaking out between brothers and cousins, and then everyone making up and clashing their pints together, spilling beer everywhere. Meanwhile, a band's playing flutes and bagpipes and guitars.

I knew those freshmen wanted to hear it, so I fed it to them, and they just lapped it up. They kept saying how they heard that's how Ireland is, and how they wanted to visit one day, and blah blah blah.

I told them they had a place to stay anytime they wanted one. And they laughed and high-fived me and patted my back. What a bunch of geniuses. And I thought Pepperdine was on the same level as the Ivy League or something. I mean, the lowest GPA for incoming freshmen is 3.8. No kidding. If I make good grades at this school, I'm going to laugh.

Most of the students, I've learned, are from California, but after that, they're mostly from Hawaii and Texas. I hadn't thought much about where all the students would come from, but that surprised me.

I've signed up for free tutoring in the student

center. Some of the upperclassman take an elective course that requires volunteer hours. Pepperdine's huge on serving. They offer this event called Project Serve where you can spend your spring break working with various nonprofits here or in foreign countries. I think that's really cool.

Anyway, I'm still just taking Uncle Mike's advice and writing about everything when something cool or different happens. While I'm here, I'll try to write two or three times a week, because I don't know what my study schedules will be like, or how long this college thing will last, and you only get to go to college once. So I want to record everything I can.

Goodnight!

BB

August 25, 1999

I might have a problem. Last night, some grad students found me camping out in the library.

I had my first exam today, so I went to bed last night around 10 p.m. The vacuum cleaners shut off around 9:30 p.m. I bunkered down. And just as I drifted off into that state of half wake and half sleep, the fluorescent lights flickered on, and two voices chattered back and forth.

Two college guys browsed through books just on the other side from where I was lying. One saw me through the shelves, turned the corner, and came toward me, while I pretended to be asleep.

He wore a collared dress shirt with a black vest, brown blazer or dinner coat or whatever you call it, and dark jeans with almond colored loafers. He was polite and confident. You can sense that in people. He had brown hair, hazel eyes, a clean-shaven face, and a nose that slightly curled up at its end. He reminded me of Darren, because Darren looked a lot like that. And when he reached me, he sat on his heels and wiggled my sleeping bag to wake me up.

He was smiling at me when I lifted my head. His friend, a slender kid with dark brown eyes and jet-black hair, wore a black hoodie and black-rimmed glasses. He stood with his weight on both feet, and his hands were tucked into the hand warmer of his hoodie. He was looking at me, and smiling, too. I think they were just curious as to what I was doing there.

"What are you doing, bro?" the kid sitting on his heels asked.

"Ah. Just getting some sleep," I said in my Irish accent.

"Did your roommate kick you out or something?" he asked.

"He's got a girl in his room, so I told him I'd sleep out."

"No couches in the lobbies?"

"There's people coming and going all night," I said. "I've got an exam tomorrow."

"Well, you're not going to get a good night's rest here. We've got a spare bed at my apartment. You can shower there in the morning and everything."

I said no thanks and that I really needed to get some rest, and that I was fine there. They said okay, and left.

They seemed really cool, but I hope they don't turn me in. We'll see how it goes. If they find me again, I guess I'll just have to say I was kicked out again.

BB

September 8, 1999

It's like academic boot camp here. I have to read a book every two weeks, in almost every class, and then write a paper on it. It's like the professors think their class is the only one I'm taking. High school didn't prepare me for this. But I didn't take high school too seriously. And I'm paying for that now.

I was down at Diedrich's coffee shop in Malibu yesterday. I go there to get away from campus because it's the only place to study if you're not in the library. And I'm already getting sick of the library. The coffee shop is easy to walk to from campus. It sits between Malibu Yogurt and Ralphs Grocery. There's a fountain in the center of the courtyard where moms bring their lapdogs and wear sunglasses like they're trying to hide the fact that they're famous or something. The children play there and birds take baths in the fountain.

Diedrich's is the kind of place where as you get close to the door, you can smell coffee and burned or scorched chocolate from the croissants. It smells really good. And everyone's friendly. It's like the neighborhood hangout.

A coffee shop is a great place to study, and people watch, and you don't feel so alone there. I figured that maybe I can become friends with some of the locals and let that be my social time. It takes time to build relationships with people. Uncle Mike gave me this book by Stephen Covey, and he wrote that it takes three months to get to know a person, and about six months to build a pretty good relationship with them so they don't think it's weird when you call them out of the blue to hang out and stuff.

Anyway, that guy who found me in the library, the one dressed like a kid from Oxford with his brown dinner coat and almond loafers, he was there reading, and he saw me before I saw him. He called out to me, and so I walked over and shook his hand. I couldn't be rude. He stood from his seat when we shook hands.

His name is Clayton "Finn" Fincannon, and his friend is Ryan. I figure that I need to be friendly to both of them so if they find me in the library again, they won't rat me out. Finn looked real peaceful and he was reading a book by Thoreau called *A Week On The Concord and Merrimack Rivers*. I think we could be good friends since he's reading Thoreau.

When Finn and I shook hands, he said, "I've been thinking about you." And I could tell he meant it in a way that wasn't weird. He asked how my back was, after sleeping on the floor. But he was being genuine, not like a jerk. So, we laughed about that, and then Ryan joined us for a coffee.

Finn was sipping on hot tea mixed with milk and honey, and Ryan drank his coffee straight black. Finn asked if I drink tea with milk and honey back in Ireland, and I said no, and he said he thought everyone did there. I recovered quickly and said my family did but I never took to it.

Finn said he spent a summer in Scotland working with homeless drug addicts, and I learned that Ryan worked with AIDS victims in East Africa. They're both at Pepperdine on full academic scholarships.

Man, they make me look bad. But I like that about them. They invited me to The Beanery tomorrow night. Apparently, it's this really cool pub in Santa Monica. I told them I wasn't twenty-one and they said you can still hang out there since they serve food.

I was feeling real lonely, and they hadn't asked me a lot of personal questions, so I said yes.

Besides, their invite means a lot because it's the first time anyone's invited me out since I've been here.

We'll see how it goes.

Goodnight!

BB

September 9, 1999

You're not going to believe this, but Finn and Ryan and I went to The Beanery and Shannon was working there! And Finn and Ryan know her! I guess that's what happens at a small school. It wasn't a complete disaster.

But man, oh man, was it good to see her again! She was so surprised and her eyes went wide and she squealed my name and ran and hugged me real tight! And I mean, it happened as soon as we walked through the door. We saw each other, and she made a beeline right to me. It was fantastic.

Finn and Ryan were watching us with these real surprised smiles. "How does this guy from Ireland know Shannon?" is what I'm sure they were thinking.

I had to lie to Shannon and tell her that I had spent the summer in Ireland and the accent wore off, but that I was pretending to be from Ireland as a joke. I pulled her aside when I told her that, so that Finn and Ryan wouldn't hear. I told her that some freshman friends and I are seeing how far we can take it. She thought it was weird but believed me.

I feel horrible for lying. Because I know I'll have to come clean at some point, probably. Unless I can think of something later. She's the last person I want to lie to, but I don't know what else to do. I don't have my life together at all. I know that. I've known that for a long time.

I told her I was accepted into Pepperdine, that I met a guy named Ian at the expo and he sang Pepperdine's praises, and I looked at pictures of it on the Internet when I got home and decided to just apply and see what happened. They offered me a full tuition academic scholarship, so I took it, and here I am. I told her I was sorry I didn't call and tell her, but that I didn't want to freak her out and make her think I was following her to Pepperdine like some kind of stalker. She said, "No! I'm glad you're here!" and I could tell she really meant it.

I asked Finn and Ryan not to let her know they found me sleeping in the library, because I was embarrassed and didn't want her worrying about me, and they understood. Then, they congratulated me on being nice enough to let my roommate make it with that girl, and that made me feel worse, because they reminded me that I was lying to them, too.

Shannon was busy working, but she said she wanted to hang out with us as soon as she could.

We didn't say we'd call each other or anything, and that's okay, because I know she was busy being a waitress. Next time we go there, she said to make sure we get a seat in her section.

Finn and Ryan said later that they see Shannon a lot at different parties, and talk to her all the time, but they had never just hung out with her and her friends on their own. They said we should all get together, and I agreed. If I can be good friends with all these people, that'll be wonderful. Shannon and I can be together, and we'll share all the same friends, and it'll be everything I ever wanted. Other than the fighters at the dojo, I've never really had any friends, except my brother Darren.

So on the way to The Beanery, I got to know Finn and Ryan more. We rode in Ryan's green Camaro, and Finn made me sit in the front, even when I tried to sit in the back. At The Beanery, the wooden floors creak and crack when you step on them. Old car tags, pro sport jerseys, Polaroid pictures, and bottle caps are nailed across the walls.

And you can order anything! Steak, chicken, burgers, salads, eggs, pancakes, anything. The wall behind the bar is covered with hundreds of beer taps. There's not a larger selection of beers anywhere in the city, they said. And they stay open real late. Until 2 a.m. I can see why Shannon wanted to work here. It's really cool. It's different from anything I've ever seen.

Finn and Ryan asked about Ireland, what it's like, and I told them about a few common things like sheep herding and the architecture of the buildings and stuff, and about the potato famine back in the 1800s. That satisfied their curiosity, and so we talked about our favorite books and movies and hobbies.

Finn and Ryan are getting their Master's degrees in literature. Finn's favorite writers are Thoreau and C.S. Lewis, and Ryan's is Ray Bradbury. Ryan's from Canada, and he likes rock and his favorite band is Dashboard Confessional. Finn said he likes everything but he listens to a lot of classical and jazz. He also likes Coldplay and Dave Matthews. Ryan is Catholic, but I don't know if Finn is religious. I didn't ask.

I said I liked trad, and explained that it is Irish traditional music. I said I also like Rage Against The Machine when I'm working out. I didn't make fun of Finn for liking classical and jazz because I thought it was different and it suits him. And I'm glad they have music they like and were willing to tell me that kind of personal stuff.

Finn likes the movie *Casablanca*. Ryan loves hockey and he really likes a movie called *Life Is Beautiful*, which he said is an Italian film. I've never heard of it. Ryan also said he liked *The Matrix* and *Fight Club*, which just came out. I haven't seen them yet. I told them my favorite movie was *Good Will Hunting*, but that's just because it's the last movie I watched, and I don't even remember when that was. But I really liked it.

Finn and Ryan said they had seen that movie, too. Finn said it was brilliant and Ryan said it was really good. And that made me feel nice because now we all have something in common. But I don't think either of these guys have been in a fight. They're not the fighting type. I'm all right with that, and I think that might be best. It will be good for me to be friends with guys who don't like to fight.

I also learned that Finn is on the lacrosse team, even though he's a grad student. He played on the undergraduate team, but didn't use up all his eligibility. Ryan has asthma, so he can't play sports or run a lot.

Right now, I'm just glad I have friends. And I'm glad they let me be myself without asking a lot of personal questions. I can't wait to hang out with Shannon again. I'm really excited! I'm excited about everything, actually.

Goodnight!
BB

September 11, 1999
Classes are in full swing, and I'm meeting every other day with a tutor. I take every book I have to read and divide it into twelve sections. And

then I read a section every day. That way, they're read two days before they're supposed to be. So I can stay ahead.

When I'm not in class or at the gym, I'm always studying, reading, writing papers, preparing for exams, all that. I didn't get the job as a trainer at Malibu Gym, but Finn told me that his coach was looking for a specialist to create workouts and dieting schedules for his lacrosse team, so I called three times, left two messages, but I never heard anything back. So, I went and visited the coach in person, unannounced, and I got the job.

It only pays $150.00 a week, which isn't a lot, but the reason they're hiring me is because they can't afford a pro. Anyway, it's not enough to save, but it's enough for me to live on and not eat up my savings. I don't eat out and I don't have a car or rent expenses, so I'm making it. Other than all that, I'm really enjoying everything. I really like most of the books we're reading in class, but sometimes I don't feel like I have enough time to digest it all. It's some heavy stuff.

The professors meet with us one-on-one if we have questions. My ethics professor, Dr. Daniels, he's really cool. Finn and Ryan like him a lot. We've read Victor Frankl's *Man's Search for Meaning*. His teachings to love, receive love, and find goals and a life purpose, have really helped me. We read Jane Austen's *Pride & Prejudice* and *The Count of Monte Cristo* by Dumas. Harold

Kushner's *When Bad Things Happen to Good People* has helped me find a lot of peace about Darren.

In theology, I'm taking this class called Introduction to Biblical Interpretation and it teaches us to study things like what time period and culture the author of each biblical book lived in, and who he was writing to, and who was receiving it, and what was going on in their culture that might have influenced how they interpreted what they had read. By studying the "political, social, religious, and economical life of the people and cultures, it gives insight into the biblical text."

I like that because I thought theology would be like Sunday school class or something where we just read the Bible and talk about it. But we're studying a lot of Middle Eastern philosophy from 1,000 BCE, which they call "The Ancient Near East." We also study a lot of archaeology, which is real fascinating to me.

The material we read, the discussions in the classrooms, our studies in the library, conversations with classmates in the classroom, and how everyone reacts differently because they're all from different states in the USA and different countries and cultures, it's really something to experience.

I thought about Shannon last night and took her ribbon out of my backpack. I fell asleep holding it in my hand. I called her last night from the library phone, and we talked a while. She has a cell phone, but I haven't bought one yet. She thinks I'm staying in the dorms, and since girls aren't allowed to be in the boys' dorms, that'll give me a good excuse not to invite her over.

I asked when we were going to hang out, and she said we would soon, but right now, she's busy with work and school and auditions, but that we'd get together ASAP. She was on her way to work at The Beanery, so I let her go. She seemed distant, but maybe she's just busy. But I'm kind of scared. I mean, I know we can't be in New York and that she has her own life here, but what if she's dating someone? I hope not.

Goodnight!

BB

September 19, 1999

Shannon's dating someone. I wish I could say that I can be happy for her, but I can't. I understand she didn't know I was coming here, and it's my own fault for not calling her and finding out if she was dating someone, and all that blah blah blah, but it still hurts.

Here's how I found out. Two nights ago, Finn and Ryan invited me to go back with them to The Beanery. So I called Shannon and told her we were coming. She said she wasn't working, but she and her friends were out on the town, and that they'd swing by. When they arrived, Shannon and I saw each other and hugged each other, and I would have held her longer, but she pulled away, like she was hugging a friend.

She said, "Brian, you need to know—" and just then, this guy with dark, wavy hair and a smooth clean face, like he had just stepped out of a shampoo commercial or something, snuck up behind Shannon and kissed the side of her neck and wrapped his arms around her waist. Man, I wanted to kill him.

I tried to pretend I wasn't shocked, but Shannon was watching my face, and she felt bad, I could tell. She didn't want me to find out that way, I know. But she introduced us. His name is Will, and he was really nice, and that made me not want to hate him as much. But I still don't like him.

Will's in an alternative rock band and he does theater on the side, and he travels a lot. After we met and shook hands, he saw someone else he knew and he yelled, "Hey Johnny! Well, you finally showed up!" and he left. Shannon explained that they had dated before she met me in New York. They broke up, but now they were back together again. Sometimes, she said, they travel together for shows. I felt like puking. You know, just thinking of her traveling with Will and probably having sex with him makes me want to puke.

I told her I understood, and I meant it, though I hate it at the same time. But I appreciate that she didn't blow me off or act awkward. That would have hurt really bad if she did. It also didn't help that she was looking so gorgeous again and her hair smelled like vanilla. She was also wearing a blue v-neck long-sleeve shirt with the number 7 in the middle, and it looked great on her.

She hung out with me and Finn and Ryan for a while, but we just talked about classes, how some were boring and others were great, and how we liked some of our professors, but didn't like others. It didn't go much deeper than that. Man, that whole conversation was just depressing. I was quiet mostly and Shannon noticed. She was as nice to me as she could be. I'm just glad she didn't leave too soon, but stayed to let me know she still cared about me as a friend.

She could have left, too. Easily. Her friends are waitresses with her, and they were over to the side, talking to Will and a bunch of guys. They weren't being rude. They just didn't know us. Then they dragged her away from us to talk. I don't know what they talked about or what they thought was so urgent. Why couldn't they have just left her alone?

At the end of the night, Shannon and I hugged, but she kept it short. I'm not having a good night, especially since I came to Pepperdine just so she and I could be together. But I'm trying to stay positive. I'm enjoying college more than I thought, and I'm glad I met Finn and Ryan and Dr.

Daniels. So I'll keep trying to let my mind dwell on those things, like all the psychology books say to do. And I'm trying to be a better person.

BB

September 27, 1999

So I thought about this and if Shannon is happy, then I'm happy she's happy. I can be her friend, and that can be enough.

I walk around Pepperdine and I see the ocean behind the green hills, and I see a lot of students dating, with their arms around each other, and I wonder if they've had just as hard of a time with love and relationships as I have.

Do they really love each other or is one of them just using the other to fill a giant hole in their soul? I wonder if it's a different story for each couple, but I really hope they're happy, and I hope they're not lying to each other, and I hope that someday I find as much happiness as they have. But I think I have a lot to work on. I mean, would I date me? I'm not sure I would.

I was in the caf the other day and Dr. Daniels stopped me and asked what I was thinking about because I was staring into my plate. I surprised myself with my question. "Why do people lie?" I asked.

He looked away a second, then looked back at me, and said, "Because of fear."

"Fear of what?"

"Fear that they can't be in control." And then he said something I'll never forget. He said, "When we lie, we're not being ourselves. And if we lie about who we are, then people can't love us for who we truly are. They love who we portrayed ourselves to be."

Ouch. Next time, he should just take a sledge-hammer to my chest. But he's right. I think about what Dr. Daniels has to go through as a teacher here. Girls wear deep v-neck t-shirts and cheer-leader shorts and I've seen male professors do everything they can to ignore their bodies and just look at them in the face. They can't say anything, I guess. Because that would mean they were looking, and then to say something might be called sexual harassment or something. And everyone likes to be offended these days. It could be easy to score some good grades if you threatened a professor with a lawsuit or some-thing.

I never want a girl to think I like her because of her body. I want her to know I like her because of who she is. I know most guys my age don't see it that way. Physically attractive girls are a dime a dozen. But to get to know her as a person, that takes some real digging.

I think that's why I care about Shannon so much. I've seen her heart, and I don't have eyes for anyone else. I just have to be patient and be a good friend to her. I really need to build her trust so that I can just be a friend to her and not act all weird. And I really need friends my age. I've always known that, but I haven't wanted to admit it.

I'd never want to do anything to hurt Shannon. Or even Finn and Ryan or Dr. Daniels. That'd kill me. I already know it would.

BB

September 29, 1999

Everyone goes to the men's basketball games here, even though Pepperdine rarely wins. The water polo team and the men's volleyball team win the national championship almost every year, but people rarely watch them.

It's funny how things work like that. When Pepperdine plays Gonzaga, their rival, the gym's packed. And Gonzaga always beats them. Gonzaga makes it to the Sweet 16 almost every year. A upperclassman told me the other day that when he was a freshman, Pepperdine beat Gonzaga, and Pepperdine students took off their shirts and painted their chests orange and blue and ran around Alumni Park.

Pepperdine's school colors are tangerine orange and navy blue because of the sunsets in Malibu. Their mascot is also a wave. No kidding. Willy the Wave. He's an electric blue cartoon surfer with giant black sunglasses and blue gel-spiked hair that folds over at the top, forming a wave. He reminds me of a Smurf-turned–Beach Boy. But he's not naked. He wears a navy blue Hawaiian shirt with white flowers in a wallpaper design, and under it orange shorts.

Talk about being original. I don't think there's a school on this whole planet with a wave as a mascot. Anyway, Finn and Ryan like to go to the basketball games. So two nights ago, I decided to go to one of their first games, which was against Loyola Marymount.

Pepperdine's gym isn't very big, so it was easy to find Finn and Ryan sitting at the top of the bleachers. About three rows down from them were these guys wearing Greek letters on their shirts, which meant they were in a fraternity.

When I started up the bleachers, I saw Shannon sitting on the bench behind Finn and Ryan. Will was beside her, but he was talking real fast and gesturing with his hands to a guy and two really hot girls beside him. Just ignoring Shannon. Man, I really can't stand that guy. Shannon smiled at me, and that made me feel real good. I'm glad she's not giving me the cold shoulder because she has a boyfriend.

I walked up and Ryan shook my hand. I shook Shannon's hand and would have hugged her, but I would have had to reach over Ryan, and that would have been awkward. Plus, I didn't want

Will to get all riled up. I'd have to break his arm and throw him down the bleachers or something.

When I shook Finn's hand, he stood an inch or so, and I appreciated that. He reminds me more of Darren everyday. I think they would've been good friends. That makes me sad and happy at the same time because it feels good to have a guy be your friend, but it makes me sad because I know I'll never know what kind of man Darren would have become.

After we shook hands, I said, "I just want you to know I'm a member of the I Felta Thigh fraternity and I wonder if you two young men would like to be our new pledges." They all looked at each other and laughed. "It's all right if you're old grad students, because it doesn't matter as long as you have money to give us the entrance fee. Are you good at sports? Can you get girls to come to our parties? You can! Well, join up right now. And you can help us drop roofies in girls' drinks, and take their pictures with their clothes off, and measure their IQ with a tire gauge."

In my side view, I saw two of the frat boys turn around and look up at me but I didn't care. Finn and Ryan laughed, but I think it was because of my accent, to think that a boy from Ireland had caught on so quickly to the Greek social club aspect of their American culture. I can be a performer sometimes. I really can. But I have no idea why I said all that. I guess I just wanted to make them laugh.

I'm really glad I can be a bit of myself with them and say stupid things like that, even though I'm lying about being from Ireland. But I do hope that one day, if they find out the truth, they won't be too angry at me. Maybe they'll give me the chance to tell them the entire story. Uncle Mike said that if we give people a chance to tell their story and we listen, we might like them more, or realize that we might have made similar decisions if we had been in their shoes.

I sat beside Ryan so I could be near Shannon. We all talked some, but Finn and Ryan were more interested in the game. That was good because it gave me some time to chat with Shannon, and then have the game to watch when Will started finally paying her attention instead of running his mouth. I mean, how could you ignore a girl like Shannon sitting beside you?

The point guard was really good. Finn had mentored him in literature last year. The wing guard was a guy named Kirk. Shannon said Kirk spent the night with her old roommate on the weekends, back when Shannon was a freshman. Apparently, it's easy to sneak people into your dorm. Her roommate was in love with Kirk, but Kirk wasn't in love with her. But he slept with her anyway because she was good in bed.

Shannon said he made her roommate call him Captain Kirk, and Kirk said she was a tom cat in the sack, and I couldn't help but start laughing, and then Shannon started laughing, but then she hid her smile with her hand because I think she felt bad about it.

Shannon didn't like Kirk at all because she had to watch her roommate cry all the time. They were really close, so it affected Shannon on a real deep level. I had my make-out sessions and mess-arounds with girls in the past, but I'm really glad I was never like Kirk. I mean what kind of guy, in all seriousness, wants to be called Captain Kirk in bed? I mean, let's just think about that for a second.

Anyway, I read in class that emotional and psychological pain is actually just as traumatic, if not more, then physical pain. It affects the brain in similar ways. Shannon said Kirk was sleeping with some other girl right now.

I wonder if Kirk makes her call him Captain Kirk, too. Apparently the girl is really materialistic and shallow, though shc has a high IQ. Shannon said Kirk tells the girl he loves her, but when Shannon sees Kirk out, he's never with that girl. He's with his pals or another girl. Thinking about all that, the whole idea started making me mad. I think it was more because it hurt Shannon in the process. Then Shannon said Kirk was in one of the more popular fraternities, and that really set me off.

After the game, we all went to The Malibu Inn. It's a popular pub and dance hall because they play club music after 11 p.m. and if you're twenty-one the drinks are good. Finn and Ryan talked about class mostly, and Will and Shannon danced a lot. That was hard to watch, but I'm glad they never played any slow music or bump-and-grind stuff. If I had to watch Will and Shannon slow dance together, him resting his head on her shoulder, or them kissing, I would have puked.

I'm a horrible dancer. I tried once in middle school after a high school football game. They called it a sock hop and made everyone take off their shoes. The floor was really hard and my feet started hurting. And one time I tripped because my left heel stepped on my right toe, and my right sock came plum off and I stumbled and landed on the dessert table and knocked an entire tray of brownies and sugar cookies onto the floor. I ran out the door because I was embarrassed, and then I came back in through the front door, and no one knew the difference.

Anyway, there at The Malibu Inn, I watched all the people dance and never went out onto the dance floor except this one time when they were playing a Michael Jackson song. And even then, I made sure Shannon wasn't there. She was in the bathroom. But I like Michael Jackson. I like "Billy Jean" and "Bad" and "Thriller", which is the song that was playing. I only went out there because Finn and Ryan got out there and danced, too. You can be a straight guy and dance with other guys to that song. It's okay. We just shook our waists and kicked our feet out to the side like Michael Jackson does. No one was grabbing their crotches.

I saw Captain Kirk out there, and he was with that girl he's been sleeping with. I asked Shannon to show me which car was his, and she pointed to a brand new black SUV sitting in the parking lot. So I left Kirk a note under the windshield that said if he didn't start treating girls at Pepperdine right, mainly my niece, I was going to have him kicked out of school.

I signed it "A Pepperdine Admin." I also wrote that I didn't think Jesus would appreciate Kirk's behavior toward girls since they're God's daughters. I was just being a smart aleck, but I know what to say after listening in theology class. Pepperdine's a Christian school, but most of the students go there because it's in Malibu, not because it's Christian. So I knew a note like that would eat at him, especially since he didn't know who left it.

I wasn't going to slash the guy's tires or break a window, though I probably would have if Shannon asked me to. But Shannon laughed and thanked me, so that went well. After that, we went to a party. Shannon said she and Will would meet me and Finn and Ryan there. The party was at a student's beach house that his parents owned. His name is Ethan, and he met us at the door wearing a house robe and holding a wooden rail that he pulled from the staircase rails leading up to the second floor of his house.

His parents were gone to a dinner party or something. But Ethan had drunk quite a bit and was playing swords with the wooden rail. He poked Finn in the chest when we stepped onto the front porch. Finn laughed and they shook hands. Ethan said everyone was out back and he hoped we'd have a good time.

A bonfire was going in the backyard, which was the beach. It's strange for me to call it a backyard when it's not grassy. It's sand. Bonfires in private backyards are real popular in Malibu. Everyone roasts marshmallows, listens to loud music, drinks a lot, and neighbors just expect it, I guess.

There was a shaggy-haired kid in cut-off khaki shorts and a hemp necklace, and he was playing Dave Matthews on his guitar. I overheard this one group saying that they were going to Berkeley this coming weekend to listen to a new kid play named John Mayer. They said he's up-and-coming. I've never heard of him.

Ethan came out back. He had just returned from a study abroad program in Italy and he brought back three bottles of red wine. He was just passing it around to all of us. There were about thirty people out there, and he said he wanted his friends to enjoy it with him, that it was his way of enjoying it, too.

And then he handed the bottle to me to take a swig. I tasted it, and it tasted really good. But I only took a sip, then thanked him and told him it was great. And I really meant it. But I didn't want to drink up all his wine. I wanted Ethan to see his friends enjoy that wine, because I believe that's what he wanted. But it really meant a lot to me that he would let me have some of his wine from Italy, and that he would treat me like a friend even though he didn't know me.

Finn and Ryan knew everyone and everyone seemed to like them a lot. We went back into the house, and I scanned the crowd for Shannon, but I didn't see her or Will yet. Then this new girl I've never seen before named Tabitha said to Finn while looking at me, "Who's your friend?" She had blonde hair and brown eyes. She didn't wear a lot of makeup, and she was cute in a sisterly kind of way. And Finn said, "This is my friend, Brian," and it meant a lot to me that Finn would call me his friend.

She shook my hand and thought it was really cool that I was from Ireland. I don't think Tabitha's interested in me. I think she was just curious. I think she likes Finn, but I can tell by the way Finn stands and talks to her that he just sees her as a friend.

Shannon came into the room behind Tabitha,

and I was really happy to see her. We hugged and said hello. Her hug was warm and lasted a second longer than the hugs she's been giving me, and that was real comforting.

I was really glad she felt comfortable enough to do that. Will and some of her friends were hanging out in another room. And just as we started talking, I heard "Hey!" from across the room. And this tall guy with a neatly trimmed strawberry blond beard and mustache started walking over to me.

He was talking to some students who knew I was from Ireland. I met him halfway, because I don't like people just running up to me like that while I'm standing still. Also, I didn't know if he might know me from Alabama or something and I didn't want people overhearing our conversation.

He introduced himself and said he was from Ireland and that his name was Aiden. He was built like a basketball player and wore black socks with white sneakers. That's very European. I see kids from Italy and Germany at Pepperdine wearing stuff like that. Aiden was very excited and asked me what part of Ireland I was from, and I told him Doolin, near Galway, and he was really excited because he said he had been in that area years ago.

I was really nervous, but I played it cool, and I told Aiden that was great, and I asked where he was from, and he said Belfast. Shannon was watching, and I told him my date was awaiting me and that I'd catch up with him later. I'm really glad he didn't ask to hang out, because the last thing I need is for us to become friends. I've already weaned off from the accent some, and I didn't see any suspicion in his eyes. Maybe that's because Belfast is in the northeast corner and Doolin is in the far west. Or maybe he was just so excited to meet someone from Ireland that he wasn't paying my accent much mind. But if he had asked, I would have just told him that it had waned.

I hope I don't run into him again. When I wasn't as excited to see him, and when I excused myself to join Shannon, I could tell it put him off some. I didn't mean to. I need to figure out a way to either avoid him or make him mad at me so that he doesn't want to hang out. I'll have to figure something out.

Ethan had said there were more drinks in the kitchen, so Shannon took my hand and said she would show me how to make a White Russian, and that we should drink one together. People were standing in the kitchen when we walked in, leaning against the drawers and cabinets, talking and sipping drinks. There were a lot of jello shots and different vodkas and whiskeys, there was beer in the fridge, and there was music, but it wasn't so loud that you couldn't have a conversation.

A CD was playing Goo Goo Dolls, Pearl Jam, and Third Eye Blind, and Shannon was breaking ice apart and dropping it in our glasses. She was smiling at me, and I believe that moment is something I'll remember for a long time. I can still hear all those songs. It was a good night.

Though Shannon and I are being just friends, and I'm trying to be completely okay with that, it's hard. It helps me to remember us in New York. I remember what we had, and it was real, and she is real, and she was watching me and smiling at me in that kitchen. She was spending time with me, and right now, that's good enough.

She also has her studies and her job as a waitress, and something inside me says not to bring up New York to her. I think if she wanted to talk about that part of us, she would have brought it up already.

While we were standing in the kitchen, we met two guys named Matt and Patrick. Matt's parents own some land out at Point Dume, which is a swimming hole below a cliff that a lot of the locals know about. People jump off the cliff and build fires below, on the rocky beaches.

They're sophomores. Patrick's from Texas and he says, "Cool, man" a lot. Matt struts like a football player and talks with a business voice, like he's a business man at a conference or something. He was pretty cool, too. When I talked to them, they really listened. They weren't looking around the room to see if there was someone better to talk to. Most guys will talk to you and keep the room in their side view in case a pretty girl walks in.

At the end of the night, I left with Finn and Ryan, while Shannon stayed behind with Will and their friends. I didn't want to think about whether or not Will would be staying the night with Shannon. I just shut it out of my mind. The thought of any-body just sleeping beside her, let alone with her, other than me, makes me really mad.

When Shannon hugged me goodbye, it was warm and nice again, and she smiled at me when we let go. She said that we shouldn't wait so long to hang out again and have drinks in people's kitchens. She can be pretty funny sometimes. I hated leaving, especially since I could hear Will in the other room saying stuff like, "Is that Timbo over there!" and "Well, look who finally showed up!"

So other than listening to Will and meeting Aiden, tonight was a good night. I hope I can be with Shannon again one day. If we have to be just friends, I'll love her from afar and I hope that can be enough. I hope.

BB

October 6, 1999

I'm living with Finn and Ryan now. It's a long story, so I'll tell you the short version.

They found me sleeping in the library again, and this time they made me stay the night in their guest bedroom. They live in Drescher Apartments on campus, in room T30, which is on the third floor. Their living room has a long window, as big as the wall, and it overlooks all of Malibu, the campus and coast. The city lights cover the valleys and mountains to the left, and lights line the coast. It looks like a necklace of lights. Very cool.

It's your typical college guys' living room, though. Bare walls. No pictures or paintings or candles or anything like you'd see in a girl's dorm. Pepperdine furnished a couch, recliner, dining room table with four chairs, and even a table to put your TV on. Ryan keeps a TV in his bedroom, but Finn hasn't owned one since he left the farm when he was eighteen.

The bathroom has two sinks and a single shower large enough for four people to stand in. No kidding. The kitchen already came with glasses, silverware, knives and bowls. A refrigerator, dishwasher, and stove are there, too. And outside, in the courtyard, there's a permanent gas grill for anyone who wants to use it.

Finn and Ryan only rent the bedrooms. Pepperdine can put anyone in their apartment. Sure, Finn and Ryan have a say in who lives there, but at the end of the day, Pepperdine needs rooms for students. Each bedroom has a twin mattress with a solid wood bed frame, a matching desk, bookshelf, nightstand, and dresser. And my window allows a view of Malibu and the ocean. I can't believe people get to go to college here.

Finn's room is next door to mine, and Ryan sleeps across the hall. Another empty room sits across from mine. The first night I stayed here, I loved the idea of having my own room, knowing I could wake in the morning and just hop across the hall to the shower, and walk around my own bedroom naked, cook supper in the kitchen, and watch the sun set over the ocean. I could do my homework and write and study at my very own desk in my very own room, in front of this window with this glorious view. Wow. Just, wow.

A few days after my first night here, Finn saw me walking to the gym for my morning shower with my backpack, and my sleeping bag was poking out. He put two and two together and confronted me about it at Diedrich's the next day. I apologized for lying. I told him most of the truth. That I was staying in the library because I couldn't afford on-campus housing and was too ashamed to say anything.

Finn talked to Ryan, and they're letting me stay in this empty bedroom. If Pepperdine places two students in their apartment, which isn't likely since we're so far into the school year, Finn said I could sleep on the couch or on his floor. That's no big deal for me. Growing up, I slept on cardboard boxes because Mom sold Darren's and my beds for drug money.

Finn said they had another apartment mate last year, but he moved off campus so he could throw parties. Pepperdine has a no alcohol policy.

They both have an electronic key to open the apartment, and when it closes, it locks. Finn is leaving his key in the fire extinguisher box outside the door so I can use it to come and go.

These guys are awesome. Though they're letting me stay for free, I know how I can contribute. I'm going to cook for them. Maybe some Irish stew and steaks, but I'll need to get a cookbook. I'm thankful Aunt Karen let me experiment in her kitchen and learn the basics.

Living with Finn and Ryan has been really cool. It's funny to watch their habits. Ryan watches hockey on his TV when he's not studying. And his door's always open. He'll close it when he knows Finn and I are studying because he yells at the TV screen a lot. His schedule's a bit more chaotic, and you never know when he's coming or going.

Finn's the opposite. He lives by routine. He gets out of bed around 8 a.m. every morning, eats a bowl of oatmeal and drinks a glass of orange juice. He works out in the gym at the bottom of campus, then runs the hill back to our apartment for his cardio. He showers, studies in the library between classes, eats lunch and dinner in the caf, and when he returns to the apartment in the evening, he studies at his desk until bedtime. Every day, the same schedule. Like clockwork. I asked him why he's so structured, and he said it's the only way he can get anything done.

We've been pulling pranks on each other. It all started a few days ago. Ryan hid in my bed and jumped out and scared me when I came in late and the lights were off. Finn busted in and they started laughing at me. And then, a few nights ago, Finn hid under my bed. And when I was folding my laundry on my bed, he barked and dug his finger nails into my ankles, like he was an attacking Doberman Pinscher or something. I about jumped ten feet high.

But I got them back. Ryan was taking a shower and he had just finished watching this news show about all these earthquakes in California. He didn't know I knew, but I could hear the newscaster from my room. The shower has a curtain instead of a door. So I walked over and shook the curtain real violently and I screamed, "Earthquake!"

Ryan let out this slow, deep bloodcurdling cry that rose from the depths of his stomach. It grew so loud I had to cover my ears. I didn't know a pair of lungs could put out that much wind. I mean, I've seen it in the horror movies, but not in real life. After it was over, he swung his head around the curtain and his hair was caked with shampoo and he screamed at me. But he started laughing a few seconds later.

For Finn, he always keeps a bowl of boiled eggs in the fridge as late night snacks. So I replaced his boiled eggs with raw eggs. So when he broke the egg on the kitchen counter, raw yolk splattered everywhere. I wasn't there when he did it but Ryan said he was and that it took a second or two for Finn to realize how that happened. When I got home, we called a truce, and haven't pranked one another since.

Sometimes I feel like I'm eight years old, and sometimes I feel like I'm eighty. I rarely feel my age. It just depends on the day. I can be real serious one minute, and real kidding the next. But being here makes me feel my age, nearly nineteen years old. And I like that.

Goodnight!

BB

October 12, 1999

Finn met a girl! Her name's Eden and he's hanging out with her a lot now. She's from Colorado Springs, and they met at a lacrosse game. Ryan is also dating a girl. Her name's Joanna. She's from New York. Finn and Ryan aren't around as much anymore because of that. So I've hung out with Matt and Patrick some while Shannon's been busy. She's on a tour right now with her theater group. It's part of her internship.

I've been to a few parties with Matt and Patrick. We went to this Halloween party and people dressed up like baseball players, vampires, and zombies. Girls dressed like she-devils and nurses with low-cut tops and tiny shorts.

There are these goody-goody kids, leaders in the student government, who believe in Pepperdine's policy that students aren't allowed to get drunk off campus. So earlier this fall these kids took video cameras to parties and pretended to be having a good time and laughing, but they were filming the drunk kids and then taking the footage to the dean's office. So now, at most of the big parties, people aren't getting hammered because they're afraid of ending up on video and having to explain to their parents why the dean has them on probation.

But it's at the smaller parties that people get trashed. They're able to monitor who comes in and who can't. They're there with their friends and they just drink all night. But the parties are starting to become the same. There are drinks, jello shots, music, girls and guys pretending not to notice each other, while hoping to go home with someone.

Some nights I've ended up crashing on one of the couches in the common room outside Matt and Patrick's dorm room. In the mornings after a party, Patrick and Matt and I will walk down to the caf and have pancakes on the balcony that overlooks the ocean. Even from the caf, there are better views than any restaurant you'll find in Malibu.

I've been making it a habit every day to eat on the balcony and watch the sun go down. Most of the other freshman are too busy playing video games or talking about stupid stuff, like how they got hammered or how they snuck this girl back into their dorm.

I really miss Finn and Ryan, and I hope to hang out with them soon. I also wonder what Shannon thinks of me since we haven't seen each other in a while. It was easy when she was at school, but now she's on the road a lot. I think my decision to let Shannon be is a good one. And that's what Finn told me the other night when I was visiting him in his room. He said sometimes the best way we can show someone we love them is to just let them be. So I'm trying that.

I see Tabitha, Finn's friend from the party, around a lot. Ryan said Tabitha has a rough story, and she wants to hang out with Finn because he's a good guy and she can trust him. Ryan said Finn's the kind of guy who Tabitha could sleep in the same bed with and she wouldn't have to worry about Finn doing anything.

Ryan said Tabitha's a really good girl, a good Christian girl, the kind who takes her faith seriously. She really does try to live it, he said. But for some reason, Ryan said Tabitha has a low self-concept.

I thought that was really sad and I wondered how I would feel if Tabitha were my sister. I've decided to make sure I'm nice to her every time I see her.

BB

October 18, 1999

School's still going well. I don't give my opinion in classroom discussions, because the students like to put things in black and white too much, and I just don't see things that way. To me, the world is mostly gray. What works in one circumstance won't necessarily work in others. But you can't tell them that. They have to figure that out themselves.

I think the professors, especially Dr. Daniels, would agree with me, but their job is to lead classroom discussions and teach students how to think. So I just write my papers and try to keep my mouth shut.

The other night, I ran into Shannon at Diedrich's. Finn and Ryan and I walked in with Tabitha, Matt, and Patrick. Shannon was studying in the corner. She was wearing black-rimmed glasses and her hair was pulled up into a French bun. Just like she wore it in New York. This time, a pencil was sticking through it, and I about died. She was so beautiful without even trying.

She was real focused in her studies, and when she looked up at me, her eyes were glazed from reading so much. It's so attractive to see a girl so dedicated to something. She was working hard, and she's passionate. I wanted to hold her and kiss her, but I couldn't. So I just smiled and walked over to her table, and hoped that was enough.

She stood and hugged me and said we should really hang out when she gets some free time, that she got back into town last night and is exhausted. She said it's hard because she's working and studying all the time, and she has Will in her life. I told her it was all right, that I understood, and we'll have plenty of time to hang out. I'm not going anywhere anytime soon.

The rest of us went outside and Ryan and I sipped hot coffee, black with a little half and half. And Finn had his hot tea with milk and honey. Tabitha copied him. Matt and Patrick ordered iced mochas. And as we talked I realized I now have a solid group of friends. And the girl I love is in the building behind us, and I can see her through the windows.

It hurt to see her apart from us, I can't lie about that, but I was glad we could talk and see each other without it being awkward. All hope isn't lost, and maybe one day we can be together again. If all these people stay my friends, and I graduate from Pepperdine, I believe I can say that I'll be the luckiest man in the world. Right now, I'm really happy and the future looks nice.

I even enjoy seeing other people enjoy life. I didn't realize how unhappy I was until I stopped being unhappy. I never thought I'd come to that place in my life since Darren died. But happiness is a wonderful feeling. It really is.

BB

November 18, 1999

Christmas is coming up and it will be good to see Uncle Mike and Aunt Karen again.

But I'm staying here for Thanksgiving. No one really goes home for Thanksgiving here unless you're from California, Finn and Ryan said, because Pepperdine doesn't give a long break. So a lot of the students get together and have Thanksgiving on campus.

It will be nice to have Thanksgiving with my friends. I told Uncle Mike and Aunt Karen that I'll be home for Christmas and said that with work and flight expenses, it's best for me to just stay here. I told them about Finn and Ryan and all my other friends, and they said they were glad that I was making friends.

They still think I'm working at Malibu Gym, and that that's where I met my new friends.

BB

• • •

November 23, 1999

Thanksgiving was really good. Finn, Ryan and Ryan's girlfriend Joanna, and I all spent the holiday at our apartment. I looked up the recipe for Irish stew in a cookbook I bought at Barnes and Noble.

It has potatoes and carrots and slow-cooked beef and peas. When I made it, I let the meat cook all night in a crock-pot. Joanna roasted a turkey, Finn made southern sweet tea, and Ryan brought red wine from Napa Valley. Finn made sure that his sweet tea was Luzianne, which he boiled at the apartment. That was the tea he grew up drinking in Tennessee.

They all thanked me and congratulated me on my cooking because the meat basically melted in their mouths. And I was really proud because I had never made Irish stew before, and I was happy I could make it taste good for my friends.

Joanna's a really sweet girl. She has brown hair and brown eyes and is always smiling and laughing. Matt and Patrick had Thanksgiving with some of their friends from the dorm. And Finn's girl, Eden, she went home to Colorado. She's Joanna's roommate, which is how Eden and Finn met.

Shannon went home to Nor Cal. She didn't invite me, and that's all right, because I didn't expect her to. I wouldn't have been able to afford the plane ticket anyway. Besides, I wouldn't want to run into Will or listen to her talk about him, or us not talk about him and know the elephant in the room is there with us the entire time.

BB

December 5, 1999

I got a chance to get to know Tabitha. She came by the apartment the other day but Finn and Ryan were gone, and I was studying math in my room. I hate math. I'm really terrible at it, and that's where my tutor helps me the most. But I answered the door, and when I told her they weren't here, she seemed really down and asked if I wanted to go somewhere.

I think she was really lonely and I know what that's like. So I said all right, and asked her where she wanted to go, and she said she didn't care. So she drove us north on PCH, along the coast, and we rolled the windows down, and the sun was beautiful and that blue ocean was just sparkling like it always does.

We ended up at a Starbucks on the other side of Malibu, past Zuma Beach, but before you get to Neptune's. I thought about Shannon and how that was her favorite coffee place. Zuma is where they filmed *Baywatch*, and it's where all the tourists go. Neptune's is the motorcycle bar that's in all the movies. It's more of a tourist burger joint but people who ride their motorcycles always stop there because that's the motorcycle-thing-to-do.

The motorcycle riders always wear blue jeans and black leather jackets with gang patches spread really big across their backs. The motorcycle men and women are always kind of hefty, too. The men have long beards and mustaches and bandanas and rubber bands tied to the ends of their beards. I wonder if they ask themselves, "How do people with interests like mine dress?" Then they go out and buy that image. Like frat boys. People can really get on my nerves sometimes. They really can.

Anyway, I ordered an iced coffee, and Tabs (Tabitha told me to call her Tabs) ordered a Iced Mocha Frappuccino Light or something like that. It's some kind of a cold coffee smoothie with whipped cream and chocolate drizzle on the top. It had one of those long names where if one of your buddies ordered it, and the barista yelled it out loud so everyone could hear it, you'd be embarrassed for him. Girls can order drinks like that and get away with it.

I took one sip of her drink and I got this big sugar rush, even though it was called Light. Then we sat down outside on the front porch that overlooks the beach.

Seagulls hovered above the beaches, waiting for fish. And couples walked hand in hand. I saw a guy wearing a Speedo and I figured he was probably French.

I had already told Tabs stuff about Ireland, so I was glad she didn't want to talk about it much. But she really has a rough story. I thought that all kids who went to Pepperdine were all rich or something and came from perfect families, where they had balls and dinner parties, and all the yards were lit with bright lights, and all the dads laughed in exaggerated tones with their business sleeves rolled up, their leather watches shining, and their pleated dress pants nicely pleated.

But I've realized that most of the students here are from all kinds of backgrounds and cultures, and most of them are taking student loans. There are rich kids, no doubt, and kids of famous people, and even royalty from small countries, but they keep a low profile. Most of the students seem pretty normal, and when I overhear conversations in the caf, some students come from families worse off than my own. But they had scholarships and really wanted to get out of town and make something of themselves. I certainly can understand that.

Tabs was kind of like that, but she came from a great family, it seemed. She just had some horrible experiences with a guy she dated. I think when people grow up in a safe environment where they're loved a lot, they're naïve to how mean and dark and manipulative other people can be. Uncle

140

Mike said that people often believe others see the world the way they do and hold the same viewpoints. That's why some people are so shocked when they meet others who disagree with them on stuff they think is so important.

Tabs is from Minnesota and has three sisters. Her parents are really good people. They're still alive, still together, and still love each other. I asked her if she knew how lucky she was to have that. She said yes. But I wonder if she really does. Until college, she's never lived without her parents or the security of knowing they will be there for her if she ever needs them.

I'm telling you, I'll never, ever be mean or rude to Tabs after hearing her story. I've never heard a story like hers.

"So what's Minnesota like?" I asked her.

"It's cold."

"I figured that."

"It was settled by a lot of people from the Scandinavian countries. The Vikings. That's why there's a lot of blond hair and blue eyes. But I wasn't kidding when I said it's cold. That's one reason why I wanted to come to Pepperdine. I wanted to study somewhere else. Get away from everything I had ever known. Start over."

"Start over?" I asked.

"Yeah, I had an abusive boyfriend. And I wanted to get away from him. I grew up in the suburbs. My dad, mom, and sisters used to eat brunch together every Sunday. We'd go to this café that made bagels and waffles from scratch. They would fold it in wax paper and put honey and cinnamon and sugar on it and hand it to you. You could order coffee or hot tea. Hot chocolate." Then she smiled. I could tell she cherished those memories. "It was a good place to grow up. What about you? Did you ever have a girlfriend?"

"I went on a few dates and kissed a few girls," I said. "But nothing serious. When I was younger, most of the girls were dramatic." I was just being honest.

"Yeah, we can be that sometimes," she said, leaning back and laughing. "But we have our good parts too." She bit her straw and winked at me. She wasn't being flirty. She was just feeling comfortable with me, and I liked that.

"Do you mind if I ask you a personal question?" I asked. She shook her head no. "It's gonna be very personal."

"Okay."

"The guy you dated. How long was it before he got abusive? Ryan said something about it."

"No, you're fine, Brian," she said. "People don't ask me those kinds of questions and I wish they did. I warn girls all the time. Girls grow up watching TV and these cartoons about how beautiful and wonderful guys are and how wonderful marriage is, and about meeting Mr. Wonderful and Prince Charming.

"Most girls I know see a guy that's rich and dresses nicely and has confidence and they think that he'll always be like that. That he'll never make mistakes or raise his voice. It's not like that at all. Jeff, the guy I dated, didn't show who he really was until about a year. And then after two years, I knew for certain who he really was. He was verbally abusive after the first year and then he started getting physical.

"He never really hit me, but he would push and shove me around. And he didn't rape me, but he wouldn't let it go until I gave in. I never intended to have sex with him. But I got sick in Jamaica with our church group. And Jeff went because I was going. We were doing some inner-city work there, working with underprivileged kids.

"I was seventeen and Jeff was eighteen. And I got sick from something I ate. Jeff was really good at fooling people. So good that he convinced our youth minister he would stay up all night with me in the hospital so everyone else could go back and get some sleep.

"During the night, he had sex with me while I was unconscious. I was a virgin at the time. Kissing was as far as I'd ever gone. The next morning, he was dancing around in the room when I woke and he said, 'Do you want to know what we did last night?' I said, 'What?' And he said, 'We had sex!' And I could feel my body. A

143

girl knows, Brian. And I started crying. And he just started laughing.

"It was a scary laugh. Like there was something crazy inside him. When we first got there, there were a bunch of little Jamaican boys that sat in my lap and ran their fingers through my hair, giving me a lot of attention. They were harmless. Like, you know, eleven- and twelve-year-old boys. And I found out later that Jeff went back to that area of the city on our last day while we were out at lunch and he beat those boys up."

Tears started coming out of her eyes and she wiped them away, unashamed, like she was used to crying in front of people. I didn't mind, of course. I was thankful she could feel that comfortable with me. "It just got worse after that," she said. "I wanted to get out but I was afraid of him. We would be together in his bedroom and he would try to force himself on me and I would say, 'No, we're not having sex' and he would shake me by grabbing my arms and growl, 'Oh yes you are!' And he would turn the music up loud.

"His parents would be in the room on the other side of the house. So I would just give in. His dad was really abusive to Jeff growing up. We came in late one night and his dad was waiting for us in the living room with a belt in his hand. And his dad just started hitting Jeff in front of me. It was because Jeff hadn't taken the garbage out.

Then he sent Jeff to his room and sat down and explained the situation to me like I was a little girl who couldn't comprehend why that kind of punishment was necessary.

"But I think Jeff's dad was jealous of him. Jeff was really good at football and had a body like the David statue. You know, the statue in Italy? Jeff was beautiful. Blond hair and bronze sun-tanned skin. These dazzling blue eyes. All the girls wanted to date him. And we'd be watching TV in the living room and his dad would take Jeff's mom by the hand and announce to every-one, 'We're going to have sex!' "

"The dad was abusive to the mom?" I asked.

"I don't think so. But it was weird. And his dad would always look into my eyes with a grin when he said it."

"Like it should be you?"

"Yeah."

"And the mom just took it?"

"What else could she do? When Jeff's dad would start beating on him, his mom would just go into the kitchen and start praying. And they went to our church, you know. My parents knew them. Of course, outside their home, they were the picture-perfect family. Until you got to know them."

"I'm sorry," I said.

"It's okay."

I realized my home life wasn't as bad as I imagined. Not when compared to Jeff's or Tabs'.

I guess everything is relative. There's always someone worse off.

"How did you get away from him?" I asked.

"I came to Pepperdine."

"Has he tried following you here?" I asked.

"No. I changed my cell number, but he got my number from my parents. He called me last week. But I told him not to call me again, and that I needed to go."

"Your parents just gave it to him?"

"Yeah. They don't know about it. My dad would kill Jeff if he found out. I've forgiven him and I'm going to try to leave it in the past. Not bring it up. I pray for him. I pray that he will get away from his dad and get involved in something that will heal him."

"It sounds like he has a lot of anger in him."

"He does."

"I'm sorry if I brought up bad memories."

"No. I'm glad you asked. It helps talking about it. Thank you." She sipped her drink and took a deep breath. "Thank you for listening."

"I'm glad you got away from Jeff," I said. "Because if he was abusive when he knew he could lose you, think about what he might have done if you guys had gotten married."

She nodded and said she had thought about that. Then, Tabs rested her hand on my forearm and rubbed and patted it. It was sisterly. I'm thankful I've made friends with someone like her.

There was this one moment, later that day, when we watched some kids fly a kite with their dad. They were all happy and they'd let their dad pick them up and hug on them. I could tell they felt safe with him. And I was happy for those kids. That their dad was out there playing with them. That they even had a dad, and that he wasn't abusive.

I heard this guy in the gym say the other day that he doesn't like listening to people's problems because he has his own problems. But I've never understood that. When people want to share things with me or tell me a personal story, I like to listen. I learn stuff, and if it's a bad story, it helps me realize my life isn't as bad as I think it is. And I feel good because I made them feel good just by listening.

It's late and I need to finish a paper by tomorrow. Goodnight!

BB

December 8, 1999

It's dead week, and I've decided to get Christmas gifts for my friends, even though no one's said anything about exchanging gifts. I don't care, though. I want to give them something. Other than Uncle Mike and Aunt Karen, they've become the only family I have.

Finn is gone more and more with Eden. I rarely

see them at our apartment. I guess they hang out at hers. She paints a lot and she and Finn go to art museums. From what I understand, she's really sophisticated and educated. I don't think she's snooty because that's not the kind of girl Finn would date. Ryan said she was a debutante and I don't know what that means. He said she was trained in etiquette, ballet, and how-to-do-dinner parties and stuff like that. High class stuff.

I don't really understand Eden, and I don't know a thing about where she came from, but Ryan paints her in a good light. He said she worked with orphans while she studied abroad in Italy two summers ago. What does "work with orphans" mean? I don't know. I just hope Finn doesn't get hurt.

And that's another thing. Finn never talks about her, or brags about her, or tries to get her to hang out with us. They just do their own thing. Just the two of them. To each his own, I guess.

Anyway, for Christmas, I made Shannon a CD with the soundtracks from *Phantom of the Opera* and *Les Miserables*. She told me once that she liked those musicals. I made a pot of Irish stew for Ryan and Finn because they liked it so much, but I covered it up in the fridge and told them it was a gift for Shannon and not to touch it.

But I plan to break it out during the Christmas party. I also baked a plate of Rocky Road brownies. We'll eat those at the party, too. I didn't know

148

what to get Matt and Patrick, so I bought them gift cards to The Beanery since Finn and Ryan and I love it so much. Matt and Patrick have never been there. The gift card is enough for both of them to have a meal and drink a beer if they want to.

I talked to a literature professor and she recommended a book by Beth Moore for Tabs. Beth Moore writes Christian books for women. I made a CD for Finn and Eden, and one for Ryan and Joanna, so they can slow dance to it. I asked a lot of girls for advice on what musicians to download for romance, and they said Jewel, Sarah McLachlan, and Chris Botti.

I found the artists on Napster and listened to their best-selling slow songs, then downloaded the ones I thought everyone would like and put them on the CDs. It took me hours but I'm glad I did it. I know what it's like to be in love, but I've never danced with Shannon. So I want Finn and Ryan to experience that with Eden and Joanna.

I've saved the songs and I hope that one day Shannon and I will dance to them, too.

Goodnight!

BB

December 12, 1999

I finished my first semester at Pepperdine with one A in English, a bunch of Bs and Cs, and then a C- in math. And yesterday, we had that party here at our apartment. I told Matt and Patrick about it. Shannon came too.

It was a party with music, not really sentimental, but we all drank beer and wine, even though we weren't suppose to on Pepperdine's campus. Joanna had to work and Eden had already left for Colorado. Sometimes I think Eden is socially awkward and maybe doesn't want to hang out with us, but Ryan doesn't believe that's the case. He thinks Finn's just real private.

At the party, Finn put on some Christmas music, with a good mix of classics like Bing Crosby, Frank Sinatra, Nat King Cole, and even the country music group Alabama.

Everyone brought some food like roasted chicken and potato chips, and then I pulled out my Irish stew. They ate it all up and patted me on the back for the excellent cuisine. After dinner, everyone was eating my brownies and I couldn't help but think how funny it would have been if I had made hash brownies and never told anyone. That would have made for a great story!

Anyway, the music was going and everyone was having a good time, and I couldn't wait any longer. I was in such a good mood seeing everyone else in a good mood, that I started just passing out my gifts to everyone right then and there, right in the middle of the party. And they all liked my gifts and thanked me, and that made me feel good.

No one looked like they felt bad for not getting me or everyone else a gift, and I was glad about that. They all really were grateful to get a gift, and I'm glad because I just wanted everybody to have a gift from me so that they'd know I care about them.

When Tabs opened hers, she jumped up and down, really happy, and her hug was almost a tackle. She loves Beth Moore. Tabs said it was Moore's latest book and she hadn't had a chance to read it. Matt and Patrick laughed at their gift, in a good way, and they said they'd use the cards. They said they'd take me with them and buy my dinner. Finn and Ryan hugged me and said their girlfriends would like the gift as well, since girls like romantic music.

Shannon read the card I made for her, which I wrote the night before. I wasn't planning on writing her anything but she meant so much to me I thought it was the right thing to do. She also liked the CD I made for her.

Finn has a notebook of art paper, which is really tall paper you can rip out of a pad, and it's more coarse than construction paper. And so I got Finn's permission and I ripped out a page and then I tore all the sides off to make it look like it was something from the eighteenth century. And I wrote Shannon a handwritten letter because everyone uses computers these days.

Finn had crimson faux wax that you stick in a glue gun, and after you heat it, you can drop it onto your letter and press a metal seal stamp into it like the Roman military leaders once did. Finn's metal seal stamp is a trellis with vines wrapping around it, and he let me use it. Making simple stuff like that means a lot to people, I think, because you're paying attention to details. Here's what I wrote Shannon:

Dear Shannon,
Being able to see you around Malibu has been a great thing for me because I enjoyed meeting you so much in New York. And I wondered if I would ever see you again. And even though we're not together, I'm all right with that, because I have always loved just being in your company. I look forward to many more months of seeing you and spending as much time with you as I can as the next chapters in our lives unfold.
    Your friend,
    Brian

I kind of like that last sentence because it relates to writing and books and stories and our personal journeys, and how our personal journeys are like stories when you review them in hindsight. And I meant to sound kind of poetic, too, there at the end, which I thought would be nice. "As the next chapters in our lives unfold." Very nice.

Shannon's the only person I wrote a card for, and she took her time reading it, and when she finished, she pressed it to her heart, smiled at me, and then hugged me and kissed my cheek. It was so nice to feel her warmth and her kiss again, even if it was just on my cheek.

After that, Shannon asked me to come to her car. She had parked along the curb, and from that view we could see that the full moon had left a milky trail across the crow-black ocean. The breeze wasn't too warm or cold. It was just right. The moon shone on her face, and it was enchanting.

Shannon gave me a wrapped gift and said, "I didn't know if we were exchanging gifts, but I wanted you to have something from me." She handed it to me and I was really surprised, and happy that she was thinking of me. I opened it and it was a leather bound journal with a leather rope that wraps around it and then you can slip the rope's end through a little hook to keep the journal shut.

And she told me that she hoped I would write a book one day, and that if I did, that I might write about us and tell our story in New York. And she said she hoped I was writing about my experiences in college because they would be some of the best times of my life. And when she said that last part, she looked away and I could tell she was choosing her words carefully.

Something tells me not to let her know that I've

already written about her. I think when the time is right, I'll tell her.

I hugged her, and we held each other a moment, and it was wonderful, and I kissed her cheek, and then she said something really cool. "Thank you for being respectful and keeping your distance." She said it because of her relationship with Will, and I knew that. And I'm not sure what happened, or why, maybe it was the moment. But I kissed her cheek again, and then I kissed her forehead, and she didn't turn her face, but leaned into me, welcoming it. Then, real soft, I kissed her neck, just below her ear.

I pulled back, because I wanted to kiss her more, but she had just said she appreciated me keeping my distance, so kissing her anymore would have been a bad idea. I really wanted to kiss her on the lips, though. And I think she sensed that. She pulled me close and buried her face in my neck and breathed in my scent.

I just let her rest her head like that until she was finished. When she pulled back, she didn't say anything. She just peck kissed my cheek, like a sister. I knew the moment was over, so I took her hand, looped it through my arm, and walked her back to the party. I know I can't tell anyone about her affection. Sometimes, the best moments are the ones you can't tell anyone about. They're just too sacred.

No matter what happens tomorrow, or for the

rest of my life, I will never forget last night and exchanging gifts with her. It was another night when I was just glad to be alive. Nights like those, when you give gifts to people and make a difference in their lives, and they let you know they care about you, and they know that you care about them, and you get to have that moment with them, you can't really ask for a better time.

I love these people. I can't imagine my life without them.

What a great night!

BB

Chapter 3

December 23, 1999

I'm back in Tuscaloosa, and there's a light snow on the ground and all the stars are out. The snow glows under the moonlight and I want to stay outside all night but it's freezing and too cold to even sit around a fire.

I will say, it's strange being back home after being gone awhile, especially since I've been living on the other side of the country. Everything looks the same, smells the same, but it feels different. I think what's different is me.

I'm spending most of my days and evenings with Uncle Mike in the dojo. When I saw Tony and some of the others, they gave me high-fives and handshakes with one-arm hugs. "How you doin', mayne? How's California?" they asked. "You gettin' wit' any of dem California girls?"

"Nah, nah," I said. I put on the mitts for Tony and let him hit around. I swung at him and let him practice his ducks. Just like the old days.

Before I left Pepperdine, Finn and Ryan asked where I was going for Christmas, and I said I had family friends in Alabama. I'm trying to enjoy my time at home, but I miss everyone back at college. I thought I had felt loneliness before, but this is the first time in my life that I'm feeling truly lonely.

I keep thinking about Shannon and our special moment. I wanted to tell her I love her, but I knew I couldn't. But I do. I love her so much it hurts. But I can't think about that right now because I know we can't be together, and that stinks.

BB

December 26, 1999
Uncle Mike and Aunt Karen's two sons and their wives and kids came over yesterday for Christmas. All the grandkids are under twelve and some of them are adopted. They get on my nerves.

Uncle Mike's sons and their wives are cool. They've known me for years and kind of treat me like family now. The men always sit in the living room and watch football while the women hang out in the dining room, eating chocolate and talking. And the kids play outside and come in sniffling with snot running out of their noses and down their top lips.

I sit in the living room with the men and watch football, but I've never liked football. I do it because they all like it and I would be weird if I stayed in my bedroom reading. And I know not to say I don't like football. Especially since I'm living in Tuscaloosa and both Mike's sons graduated from Alabama. They'd think I'm gay.

They wouldn't say it but I know they'd think it. That's the thing about men. If a bunch of them are together, and you don't like the same things they do, they think you're gay.

I don't have anything against gay people. To each his own. And I don't have anything against weird people, either. I mean, I think I'm the weirdest guy I know.

Anyway, after everyone left, I started feeling lonely again, so I borrowed Uncle Mike's truck and drove to the cemetery to see Darren's grave. I haven't done that in years. I used to go there a lot when I was a kid, but over time, it just became useless, because it's just a block of cement with his name on it. Sure, his body is buried there, but it's not him. It's just his vessel.

I don't understand why people have open caskets at funerals. Because the dead body doesn't even look like the same person. And I know I wish I could forget what Darren looked like in his casket. At the grave, I talked about my life in California and how I was really enjoying it there, and that Finn reminds me of him.

When I'm there, I like to walk around and read the tombstones and I wonder what those people were like when they were alive, through all stages of their life, and if we had met, would we have been good friends. I wonder if they looked back on their life when they were older and were happy with the life they had lived.

I really hope they were happy, and that more hopes and dreams came true for them than didn't. I hope they didn't suffer much in life, and if they did, I hope it didn't last long. I hope they learned something from the pain, and that it made them better in the long run.

That was something Finn told me the other day. He said it isn't the suffering and pain we're thankful for. We're never thankful for that. But we are thankful for the lessons those experiences taught us. I like that. I could have done without a lot of the experiences in my life, but I also know they turned me into the person I am now.

Anyway, visiting the graveyard reminds me that my life will end one day, and it helps me keep things in a good perspective. I won't be here forever, so I need to make sure I don't live thinking I will.

Goodnight!

BB

January 1, 2000

Last night was another New Year's Eve party in town but I didn't go because they're always overrated. I've been to a few and they're never a good time. It's always better when it's a Thanksgiving or Christmas party because everyone knows each other. New Year's Eve parties are more about strangers and there's always a lot of loud music and drinking and all the single people are wishing they could go home with somebody and not be lonely anymore.

So I just stayed home and ate a bowl of vanilla ice cream. Uncle Mike still hides it in the back of the freezer. I also did the dumb thing of dwelling on all the bad things that have happened in my life instead of being thankful and reminding myself of the good and beautiful that's in the world.

For example, I now have very good friends in college, but I'm afraid that if they found out who I really was, they wouldn't want to be my friends anymore. And I think about Darren, too. How much I miss him, and I wonder what he'd be like now, if he was still alive, what he'd be doing for a living, and if he would be married, and if I'd like his wife.

I think about all the couples and married people, and how so many of them know each other so well and have still decided to be dedicated to each other and love each other. I long for that in my own life, especially with Shannon. I'm really happy for those couples and I try to think about them and their happiness when I feel sad. I just hope I can have that happiness one day, too.

Dr. Daniels said in class that even married people get lonely. That marriage or being a couple doesn't cure loneliness. That's hard to believe, but it's given me something to think about.

BB

• • •

January 15, 2000

I'm back at Pepperdine and it's so good to be at a place where I feel like I'm home. Shannon told me her schedule, and so I purposefully bumped into her on campus. She was sitting and sipping coffee by the fountain, waiting for her next class and looking over some notes. I knew she'd be there because she had two classes, back to back, in the Applebee Center. That's a main building on campus, and it's beside the fountain.

The fountain has a big water shoot in the middle. It shoots way up, like ten feet high. And it's encircled by a bunch of shorter shoots, so there's water constantly shooting up and pounding the concrete below. It makes a nice sound. There are benches around it, and students sit and hang out there between classes.

When Shannon saw me, she set her notes down and hugged me. It was the first time we've seen each other since Christmas. We talked a good while and I could tell she was glad I was there. It probably helped that I didn't bother her with phone calls over the holidays, and I think she knows she can trust me, that I won't be a bother to her if she needs me to leave her alone. Trust is always important.

During our conversation, she said her mom had a stroke right after the summer. So, she moved home to Nor Cal for two months, and people at The Beanery still let her keep her job. She's been stressed and gone a lot, and I hope me being back in her life doesn't cause her to get confused. Girls hate being confused. She has a lot on her mind and plate.

She didn't go into details and I didn't press the issue, but she said her mom lost all feeling on the left side of her body and needed round-the-clock care for over a month. They had a nurse for a while, but now her dad is helping. Shannon said they're adjusting, but it's not easy. I told her I was really sorry. She said it's life.

I really hope Mrs. LaFarre does well and that Shannon can do what she needs to do and not feel sad or stressed.

BB

January 27, 2000
The other day, we were hanging out in the caf. Finn, Ryan and Joanna, Tabs, Matt and Patrick and me. Shannon even joined us for a few minutes, but that was because she saw all of us eating while she was buying a yogurt to go.

We talked about what we were learning in class. In theology, I turned in a paper I wrote on St. Patrick. He was actually from England and had been sold as a slave to the Irish. Most of his family was killed. He escaped, and just as he returned home to England, he had a dream where a celestial being told him to return to Ireland and become a missionary. So St. Patrick joined the Catholic Church and started the very first school in Ireland, teaching students how to read.

Dr. Daniels said my writing has improved a lot, that it's like I'm a different person. I got an A- on the paper.

As I was listening to my friends, and talking without being a know-it-all, I saw Shannon watching me every now and then with a small smile on her face. That made me feel good, because it reminded me that she's still okay with us hanging out as friends, even though she's with Will.

BB

February 2, 2000

I visited Dr. Daniels during his office hours and we talked about what I learned in class about the importance of listening to people's stories before making judgments about them. But it was cool because it was the first time I ever just sat down with a teacher and shot the bull with him.

What I like about Dr. Daniels is that he wants to know what we think after we read the material, rather than just standing up there lecturing and spoon-feeding us.

I hated high school. I hated most of the books

we read and all the work we had to do. I think that if I could have chosen the books we read or if there were more subjects to choose from, I might have had a better time. Here at Pepperdine, I've been introduced to all kinds of writers and philosophers and psychologists, opening my mind to questions I've never even thought to ask. And I'm maintaining my grades, so I'm doing well, I think.

Dr. Daniels has a Native American or a Latino background. I'm not sure which. And he has two sons and two daughters who have done really well. When they were younger, they would do humanitarian work in third world countries as a family. Medical missions, disaster relief. They traveled the world together. I asked him what he wants to do next, and he said he's doing it, that being a professor is what he loves, and he doesn't mind doing it for the rest of his life.

I really like him a lot and I'm enjoying college more than I ever thought possible.

BB

February 10, 2000

I think I've got myself into a bit of trouble. Yesterday, that Irish kid, Aiden, from the party at Ethan's, stopped me on the sidewalk outside the caf, and he asked me about Doolin, and what I missed about Ireland, so I just made it up as I went along.

And then Aiden commented on how my accent was struggling. I said I was trying to lose the accent and sound more American because when you're in Rome, do as the Romans. And he didn't like that. He said I should be proud of my heritage. But I just shrugged my shoulders.

He got mad and walked away. After he was a ways off, he looked back over his shoulder at me, and I could tell he was trying to figure me out. And that bothers me. I'll have to be on my guard from now on. I'll avoid him the best I can.

It also scares me because things are going so well with all my friends and Shannon, and I have this deep fear that Aiden is going to mess it all up.

BB

February 11, 2000

So Aiden has been following me around some. And he keeps a suspicious eye on me. Today he was watching me in the caf, sitting with his arms crossed and leaning back in his chair.

He had this traumatized look on his face like I had done him and all of Ireland wrong. But I don't think it's because of my statement. I think he suspects something. I mean, why wouldn't I want to hang out with other people from Ireland, since that's my home? I know it's not likely for him to figure me out, but he seems like a sharp guy.

I know I'm dwelling on the worst-case scenario,

but it is a scenario. It's possible he might find out about me. And Uncle Mike always taught us to prepare for the worst but hope for the best.

I don't know how he could know, except by going to the international student affairs office and asking about me, but they'd probably dismiss him and not let him look at any official documents. But what if he points something out to them that he's noticed about me, and they look at my records and see something they missed? Or what if he knows them well and they let him take a look? He's got me worried.

I was sitting at the table with Finn and Ryan and Tabs and Shannon. And I nodded my head at Aiden and said, "Aiden keeps staring at me," and they all of course looked at him at the same time, as I hoped they would, and Aiden bounced his eyes. Then he started staring at the people at his table, but I could tell he was keeping me in his peripherals.

Finn said he might have a crush on me. We all laughed and I just went with it. I said, "The thing about gay guys is, even if they know you're not gay and they like you, they hope that maybe you are and you just don't want to admit it yet. So they'll flirt and stare at you and maybe even pat your head or something when they're really drunk."

Then they all started laughing and Finn said it sounded like I knew that from experience. But I laughed and said it was something I read in *The Catcher in the Rye*. Toward the end of the book, Holden's trusted mentor, who's been married for forty years, has been drinking. Holden falls asleep on the mentor's couch, and Holden wakes up in the middle of the night to his drunk mentor patting him on the head. And so Holden bolts out.

That freaked me out, and I wasn't even there. I mean, I was just reading about it and it gave me the willies.

Shannon laughed and said she understood why Aiden might like me, and then she winked, and that made me feel real good. I know I'm not the most handsome guy in the world, but it feels good when the woman you love flirts with you some.

I feel bad for making fun of Aiden and all that, but I have to figure out a way to get him off my back. But one thing's for sure, hopefully Aiden realizes I'm not going to be a victim. The last thing I need to do is act guilty of something. I certainly don't think this is the end of the problem, but at least Aiden's getting a good fight from my end.

BB

February 15, 2000

I found Shannon again between classes while she was sitting beside the fountain. She teasingly asked me how things were going with Aiden. I really hope she's jealous, but I can't tell if she is or isn't.

I think it's good for her to know I might be on someone else's radar, and that I might not always be around for her picking, even if it's a gay guy. Shannon told me to make sure I didn't lead Aiden on and break his heart, and I really think she might've been serious. But I laughed and told her I wasn't interested in Aiden, but that I'd be careful with *his* tender heart.

That made her smile and I capitalized on that, since I was on such a funny and charming roll. I said how can I possibly have eyes for Aiden after such a wonderful experience with her in New York.

Shannon's face went pink. She looked away, clucked her tongue and backhanded my chest, playfully. Yeah, I thought that was pretty smooth. If there are any walls surrounding that heart of hers, I think I'm taking down one brick at a time. At least I hope so.

BB

February 20, 2000

Finn, Ryan, Shannon, Matt, and Patrick and I were all at Diedrich's last night. Will's on the road with his band, and I'm not complaining. I had called Shannon and invited her. I'm glad she came, and that she wanted to.

Finn left early to meet up with Eden. I used to

think Eden intentionally stayed away from our group, but now I think Finn keeps her away. I'm not sure why. I asked Ryan about it and he said that Finn dated a girl during his undergraduate years and her girlfriends were the main reason they broke up. They didn't know Finn and they were whispering doubts into the girl's ears because she wasn't hanging out with them anymore. Or something like that. That makes me sad if it's true.

Ryan left early to meet up with Joanna, and that left me alone with Shannon and Matt and Patrick. Tabs wasn't there because Finn said she's seeing a guy she met at a party. I hope he's good to her.

Later, Aiden walked in, and he glared at me but I rolled my eyes. I'm trying to figure out a way to push him away for good so he won't want to come around me anymore. I have absolutely no idea what I need to do. And that bothers me to death.

Shannon wasn't in a talkative mood but that was all right because Matt and Patrick were goofing off and being our entertainment. Shannon is distracted and quiet a lot. I think it has to do with her mom back home. Sometimes I think Shannon feels guilty for going to school and enjoying her life in Malibu while her mom suffers with only her dad to take care of her.

There's nothing I can say or do to help, and I

know that Shannon should never feel guilty for living her life, so I just stay close by her as a friend because I know that's what she needs right now.

We read a book in class called *A Grief Observed* and the writer said that when he was mourning the death of his wife, he wanted his friends near him and talking among themselves, but he didn't want them to talk to him. He didn't want them to leave, either. He just liked them being there.

I'm not exactly sure why that is, but it's nice to know that I don't have to know the right words to say when my friends are hurting. I can just be there for them.

BB

February 25, 2000

I was in my room today, and the sun was shining on my desk, and I was reading some Thoreau that Finn let me borrow. Actually, he said I can read any of his books anytime, so I just went into his room while he was gone and grabbed that book, *A Week on the Concord and Merrimack Rivers*.

It's not Thoreau's most popular piece, but I really like it. He and his friend built a raft and floated down the river for an entire week. And when they wanted to eat, they just pulled over to the banks, built a fire, cooked their food in a pan, and slept in a tent. Thoreau describes everything they saw and his writing is real descriptive. I'm trying more and more to write like that.

Finn came in later, and I was really surprised because I haven't seen him in a while. He said Eden was studying for a major exam, and he had finished all of his work for the week, and he wanted to know if I wanted to hang out. He said if I wanted, he would show me how to catch and throw a lacrosse ball.

So we went to a place called Westward Beach near Zuma, and Finn brought his crosse and an extra one, and he taught me how to throw and catch. It's really hard to scoop the ball off the ground but I learned fast and had a real good time with it. He would take off running like you do when you're about to catch a long pass in football, and I'd launch the ball to him, but I usually overthrew it.

He wouldn't get mad, though. He just laughed, and I'd yell, "Sorry!" and he would say it's okay because it's my first time. But he said I was doing great. I'm not sure I believed him. I think he was just being nice. But we tossed the ball back and forth for about thirty minutes and then we ate a burger at Neptune's, which is that motorcycle bar.

We started talking and Ryan was right. Finn has been keeping Eden away from his friends because he said he likes that special time to just stay between them. She understands, too. And he hasn't hung out with her friends, either. He said she got mad at him once because he didn't want her talking to her girlfriends about him. I understand his past, but I think he's trying to control things too much.

Finn said he read a study saying that the human brain doesn't completely develop until around the age of twenty-four. And he noticed that it's at about twenty-four or twenty-five when people began knowing themselves and becoming the people they're meant to be. Until then everyone is still trying to figure themselves out. I don't think Finn means that people somehow have it all together by twenty-five, but they sure don't have it together before twenty-five, either.

He said when we're young, we're still too influenced by the opinions and advice of friends. He said most people don't consult older, wiser people. They go to their friends for advice and people who really don't know anything.

I'm not sure what I think about all that, but what I do know is that Finn is scared of getting hurt again. I think that's what this is all about. I don't blame him for that, but I think it's sad. That girl from his past must've hurt him real bad. Because it was three years ago and every now and then, he'll still reference it.

Finn said he would spend time with Eden's friends later, when the time was right, but now they were still getting to know each other. I still think it's controlling. He's trying too hard.

During our conversation, he was being so open and honest with me, and I felt bad sitting there and talking to him in my fake Irish accent. I've toned it down a lot and I blame it on spending so much time in California. But I'm still being fake, always lying to him and my friends. That's the thing. Every time I talk to my friends, every time I open my mouth, I'm lying.

Shannon thinks it's a joke, and my friends think it's real. I almost told Finn I wasn't from Ireland right then and there. But I decided not to. I think one day, and it might be soon if Aiden keeps at it, I'll have to come clean about who I am. And I'm trying to figure out how to do that and not hurt my friends or get into a lot of trouble with Pepperdine. But I don't think avoiding trouble is possible.

If I come clean about who I really am, and Finn and Ryan don't want to be my friends anymore, I don't know how I'll handle that.

BB

March 6, 2000

I had another run-in with Aiden today, and yesterday Shannon dug deeper into this so-called story that I'm Irish, and I about snapped.

I was at Diedrich's studying and Aiden came in and walked right up to me. I was reading for class, and Aiden looked determined, as if he came into that coffee shop just to find me. His eyes were wide and fixated on me and he said he couldn't stop thinking about how I didn't want to speak Irish anymore.

I almost laughed, at first. But then I shot out of my chair and got in his face and told him to never talk to me like that again, and to stay away from me, because I have bad memories back home and I'm trying to forget them.

And then I threw a zinger, which I probably shouldn't have, because it really set him off. But that was also my point. I told him I believed that if Ireland had just let the English rule, then our people wouldn't have been massacred and starved to death. And if it was up to me, the English would have never been kicked out.

Of course I don't believe any of that, and if someone from Ireland read this journal, I'd die from shame. But I had to think of something to get rid of him, and nothing else has been working.

Aiden got so mad he punched the door on his way out and the manager chased him down and said he wasn't allowed to come to Diedrich's anymore. His face was as red as a beet and he was yelling about me and pointing in my direction. But I couldn't understand what he was saying because his speech was slurred and this was all through closed windows. He was that mad, and I don't blame him one bit.

And then today, I was hanging out with Finn and Ryan and Joanna beside the picnic tables, and I was speaking in my Irish accent. It was just the three of us, and then Shannon walked up and I couldn't stop the accent. Shannon smiled and said that now we were alone, what's this joke about the accent?

I thought she'd blown my cover, so I just told her it was a long story, and I'd tell her the whole thing later. Just as she asked, luckily, Eden walked up and Finn ran over to meet her. Their plans for the weekend involved Ryan and Joanna, so they were all distracted.

They're going to the Hearst Castle this weekend. They invited me, but I don't want to be a fifth wheel, and I can't invite Shannon out no matter how much I want to. Besides, Will's back in town, and I'm sure they'll be hanging out and having sex, and that makes me sick.

Anyway, all this really got my brain working and put me through all these guilt trips. I haven't slept well the last two nights. If Darren were here, he'd know what to do. I'd ask Finn or Dr. Daniels, but I can't, of course.

I don't know how much longer I can keep all this up. It's causing mental stress I didn't anticipate, and I just don't like it anymore. It's getting worse. I feel like I'm having to lie to cover up other lies, which means I'm just lying and lying and lying, and it's all spinning out of control.

That's all. I need to try and get some sleep.

BB

• • •

March 28, 2000

So last week, Aiden and one of his Irish friends from the party trailed me on the sidewalk outside the caf, and Aiden said he didn't think I was from Ireland. His friend kept quiet, probably wondering if Aiden might be onto something.

Aiden was bombarding me with all these questions like how come he only sees me wear American style clothes, and asked me what county Doolin is in, and what was the name of Ireland's last three prime ministers. Finally, I just turned around and dropped my bag and told him if he kept at it, I was going to knock his teeth out.

Aiden backed off and kind of smirked, but his friend just looked at me, like he was trying to figure me out. What Aiden will do next, I don't know.

Last night, I baked ground beef with potatoes and carrots for Finn and Ryan, and we ate and drank sweet tea by the living room window that overlooks the ocean. It was beautiful, and they were saying some funny things, but I can't remember it all because I was distracted about Aiden.

I think I'm going to tell Finn the truth and see what his advice is for me. I've gotten to know him and Ryan pretty well, and they're the most nonjudgmental guys I know. I really hope they'll understand.

BB

• • •

April 7, 2000

This confession didn't go as well as I hoped, but I did it. It feels a lot better, but the you-know-what hit the fan.

Last week, I told Finn who I was. It was at night and Ryan was out with Joanna. Finn was in his room folding laundry on his bed. We asked about each other's day and then I told him I needed to tell him something real important.

He looked at me and realized I was serious. Then he bit a smile and said, "Uh-oh. Do I want to know?"

"Probably not," I said. "But I need to tell you anyway. I'm not from Ireland."

"You're not from Ireland," he said, and it was more of a confirmation rather than a question.

"No."

He bit back a grin and said, "Okay. Well, where are you from?"

I thought he'd just go back to folding socks or something while I explained away, but he didn't. He stopped and stared at me. So, I spilled it. I told him everything, but gave him the real short version.

I didn't tell him about Darren, but I told him I came from a poor family in Alabama, that I got in trouble with the sheriff and how that kept me from being eligible for scholarships and grants. I told him about the Os Guinness Scholarship, how I lied about my citizenship, and how I hired that Irish girl on Elance to mail in those documents for me.

Finn started laughing. That really surprised me. "You're joking," he said. He thought I was pulling another prank on him. But I didn't laugh, and when he realized I was serious, he stopped. "But everything else is true? You don't have a split personality or anything?"

"No," I said. And I still wasn't smiling because deep down I was afraid Finn would get mad and hate me or something.

He sat down on his bed and chuckled. Then he looked back up at me. With a curious smile, he said, "Tell me all about it."

"What do you mean?" I asked.

"Well, you've got my interest now. Take me from you hearing about the scholarship, to up to now, this moment, right now. I want to hear every detail."

I think he wanted to make sure that was the only lie I had spun. So I told him the rest. Everything from hearing about the scholarship, to working at the dojo, to meeting Shannon in New York. "But I can't tell anyone else yet," I said.

"I won't tell anyone," Finn said.

"What do you think will happen when Pepperdine finds out?"

"I don't know," he said. "But the longer you wait, the worse it'll be."

He started folding his laundry again, but he stopped smiling. And he didn't smile any more after that. I think it started sinking in that I had been lying to him this entire time. He probably thinks he can't trust me like he used to. That's what I'd be thinking.

"You think so?" I asked.

"Probably," he said. He was quiet a second, and then he got started. "But if you decide to tell them who you are, I know Dr. Daniels is being promoted to the Dean of Students next year and could probably help. He's a professional here and will have to make responsible decisions with the news. But I can talk to him for you."

"That would be great. What about Ryan?"

"You should tell him. If he finds out later and learns I knew the entire time, he might not appreciate that."

"What about Shannon?" I asked, more panicky. "She'll think I'm a liar."

"You are a liar, Brian," Finn said, and he smiled a little, but I knew he was serious, too. "I'm not saying you're a bad guy, but you lied."

"I know," I answered, and then I sat on his bed. "But what about Shannon? Back in New York, she said she hated liars. As far as I know, whatever I tell her after I confess, you know, to defend what I did, she'll probably think I'm just lying again."

"Not necessarily. Just tell her your story. Tell her everything you told me. Don't hold anything back. Don't assume you know how she'll react. Let her decide. But I wouldn't do it over the phone. I'd tell her face to face."

"What if that doesn't work?" I asked. "What if, when she finds out who I really am, it makes it worse?"

"Well, don't assume anything. Don't make her decision for her because you're afraid of rejection. I wouldn't wait any longer. If you're ready to come clean with her, and you know you love her and want to be with her, you need to tell her."

Finn's right. I know he is. Now I need to muster up the courage to do it. When I left his room, I stopped and said, "Hey Finn."

"Yeah?"

"I'm sorry I lied."

"I know." Then he smiled, and I could tell he believed me.

As far as Ryan goes, Finn told Ryan before I could. Ryan took it better than Finn. He actually thought it was funny the entire time. When I got back to the apartment tonight, Ryan was there and he laughed and hugged me, and he said, "Welcome home, Brian from Alabama!"

Finn added that from now on, he would call me Oz after Os Guinness, because Finn thought Os was spelled and pronounced Oz. I thought about correcting him, but decided to just let it go.

I hope Shannon's reaction is good, too.

BB

• • •

April 8, 2000

Shannon's reaction wasn't good. I saw her in the caf line, and I pulled her aside and told her what I told Finn. But I didn't give her a warning. Not even a set-up. Not even a, "Hey I've got some-thing real important to tell you. Do you have a second?" Nope. I just said, "Hey, I'm sorry but I just want you to know that I've been telling everyone I'm from Ireland because of a scholarship I needed." I mean, I delivered the news like I was ripping off a Band-Aid.

I did say that I was sorry for lying to her, and that I couldn't confess to Pepperdine yet because the timing was bad. Shannon didn't say anything. She chuckled at first, initially, when I told her. But then after a second or two, she stormed off. She probably thinks I'm a freak.

I should've been more sensitive but I thought that I would've received a similar reaction from her as I had from Finn and Ryan.

Over dinner, I told Finn about how Shannon reacted, and he and I both agreed that Shannon probably wouldn't turn me in or talk to the administration, but it would be best if I stayed away from her for awhile and let her cool off. Finn is back to treating me like he always has, which means we're getting back to the place we were. But I catch him looking at me every now and then likes he's getting to know me all over again. And I'm really happy about that. I'm sorry I lied to them all, but what's done is done and I want to make sure I don't do anything stupid in the future.

I needed to get my mind off it all, and Finn knew that, so Ryan let us borrow his car while he studied, and Finn and I drove out to Point Dume, that cliff just off PCH where during the day, you can watch the surfers below, and at night, there's a clear sight of the moon, stars, and the white fizzy waves.

We parked on the side of the road and sat out at Point Dume and talked. Finn told me about life during his undergraduate years, and how much he missed his grandpa back home in Tennessee. I didn't know this, but Finn is actually an orphan. His parents and older brother were killed in a car accident when Finn was just a toddler. His grandfather raised him.

That made me feel real sad, but it made sense. Finn has an old soul feeling about him, and we've been learning in class that pain makes people grow up faster, probably because it makes them act more like adults and they're no longer sheltered from the world. I told him that maybe that's why I only wanted to hang out with older people growing up, and Finn said no, that I was just really screwed up. He said it playfully, and we had a good laugh. But I think he meant it, too.

Finn keeps watching my eyes, but I think it's

because he's just reacquainting himself with the Brian who doesn't speak with the Irish accent anymore.

When we got back to the apartment, Ryan's door was shut and I heard Joanna giggling from inside. Before Finn went to his room, he said, "It's good to know the real you." And I don't think I'll ever forget that.

"I'm glad to be the real me, too." And just as he crossed his threshold, I said, "Hey Finn!"

"Yeah?"

"Thanks for your friendship."

And he smiled and said, "No problem."

I shut my door and turned off the lights, walked over to the window, looked out at the ocean and the full moon and stars, and thought about where all I've been and what all I've seen.

I hope I can mend things with Shannon, and that when I make my confession to Pepperdine, they'll go easy on me, and that Dr. Daniels won't think badly of me, either.

I'll say this, though. It feels good to be honest, and to let people know who I truly am. It really does.

BB

April 11, 2000

I haven't seen anyone around much. Finn and Ryan are with their girlfriends, Tabs is with her boyfriend, and Matt and Patrick have been hanging out with guys in their dorm. I haven't tried reaching out to Shannon. Finn said to give her some time, and I agree.

Dr. Daniels has us reading a book called *The Wounded Healer*. He said we should think about how we can use our wounds, the bad things that happened to us in our pasts, to help others. That this exercise of service will bring healing to us and to others, and it'll better the world.

I was feeling lonely and uncertain about the future, because I know I need to go to Dr. Daniels and confess what's happened. I didn't want to sit and wallow in my misery, so I went for a hike on one of the hills behind Pepperdine.

At the top, the hill opens to a grassy pasture about half the size of a football field. To the left you can see Los Angeles, to the right you can see the rocky bluffs along the west coast and the waves crashing against their banks. The sky was overcast, and the ocean was a dull blue. I sat down and I must have watched it all for an hour.

I can't help but think about what will happen after I confess to Pepperdine. I can't believe I'll be rewarded for my creativity, or that they'll take it easy on me and just let me keep the scholarship. And I don't even want to imagine the worst that could happen. But deep down, I'm really sensing that something worse is coming. I don't know why I feel that way, and I don't have the slightest clue about what dark night is coming, but I feel one coming on.

I've never felt this before, so maybe it's just feelings, but I'm scared I'm being prepared to face something horrible. I just hope whatever it is, I'll have the courage and patience to push through it.

BB

April 13, 2000

It's Monday, and I'm seeing the students and faculty differently. So this is post-confession life. I wonder if the students know how fortunate they are to attend a school like this, but more so, attending it while not having to act like they're someone else. I wonder if they know how beautiful it is to have friends who really love them for who they are.

I see them out and about and I wonder which ones are planning out their careers, and which ones don't have a clue about what they want to do. I wonder if they're happy here or wish they had chosen a different university. I wonder if they feel like they belong, or if they're as lonely as I am sometimes.

I see couples and I wonder how long they will last, if they will get married or break up and find someone else after college. I know that boys and girls aren't supposed to be in each other's dorms after 11 p.m., but I wonder how often they sneak in anyway, maybe through windows, or if someone leaves a sock in the door so it doesn't close and lock.

Today, I was thinking about Shannon and how much I miss her, and how I feel like I've ruined everything. So I decided to go to Diedrich's and buy a coffee, because I was feeling real lonely.

When I got there, three little kids were chasing a loose puppy while two moms wearing sunglasses watched and laughed. Birds were playing in the fountain, and two grandfather-aged men were playing chess.

Then I felt even lonelier because I didn't have anyone to talk to. But I saw this one man over fifty wearing thick glasses and reading a newspaper. His black hair was matted down and combed to the side. I've seen him around some, always sipping coffee and smoking a hand-rolled cigarette. So I walked over to him and introduced myself.

I asked if I could try one of his cigarettes, so he rolled me one, and I offered him a dollar, but he wouldn't take it. He invited me to sit beside him, so I had my first coffee with a cigarette. I actually liked it. I know it's not good for me, and I'll probably never do it again because I want to stay in shape, but I get what the fuss is about. Coffee and cigarettes. It's nice. It really is.

His name's Vinny and he made his living as a

model and talent scout. Now, he's divorced and retired and living in an RV in the Ralphs Grocery Store parking lot. I mean, he can stand up, walk over to his house, and never pay rent. And he can go anywhere he wants. Like on trips up the west coast to Oregon and Washington.

And he sure liked to talk to a youngster who'd listen to him. I mean, I could barely get a word in. He was a real chatterbox. I wondered if that's a sign he's lonely. I didn't have anyone else to talk to, so I just sat there and listened.

Vinny wanted to know what men his age usually want to know when they meet me for the first time. Like where was I from, what was I studying, did I have a girlfriend, and blah blah blah. But one of the things I remember him saying, which really stood out to me, was, "If you like to travel, then marry a girl who also likes to travel, or marry a girl who's traveled. Because once you've traveled, and you marry a girl who hasn't, she'll want to travel, and you'll want to stay home."

I feel bad because that's all I really remember. When I left, I think I made him mad. Because he was talking the entire time, and he wouldn't let me talk unless I was answering a question. He would even interrupt me while I was answering his questions. So after he was talking for awhile about the woman he was married to, and how she suffered from manic depression, and how they never had kids, and how he sold his home in Santa

Monica, was debt-free, had some good retirement saved up, and was now living in that RV, I blurted, "Hey, do you ever get lonely?"

I really wanted to know. I wasn't being a smart aleck. I just wanted to know if he got lonely at his age. Because I get lonely all the time and I was wondering if it's something I can grow out of. But he just got real quiet and stared at me, and then he said, "I think you need to leave."

I guess he thought I was crazy, or something. Are you not allowed to ask personal questions like that in Malibu? Or maybe something else was going on in his life and I hit a sore spot. You never know with people. You really don't.

So I said all right, and I left, still sipping on what was left of my coffee. I still had that cigarette, too. It wasn't like I could put it out against my shoe in front of him, or return it to him, or ask if he wanted it back. All that stuff would have been ruder, I think. But I'm glad he didn't ask for me to give it back because it was partially smoked. And that would've been awkward.

What made it worse is that after he asked me to leave, I felt even lonelier. And I'm beginning to wonder if something is terribly wrong with me. So I just came back to the apartment and read Thoreau until I got a headache. Then I went for a run and came back and showered. Now I'm going to bed.

BB

• • •

April 14, 2000
I found out from Finn this morning that Tabs and her boyfriend David have been sleeping together and he's been getting pretty rough with her. Finn said about a week ago some blue hand prints were on Tabs' right forearm. Finn pointed it out and asked her about it, and Tabs said she and David were working it out.

Since Tabs didn't ask for it to get that rough, and it's obvious it wasn't mutual consent, it doesn't take a genius to figure out that David's being abusive. For the last few days, Finn said Tabs has been elusive, hanging her head a lot, not wanting to talk much.

Finn believes David isn't just being abusive in the bedroom, but other times as well. I asked Finn what we should do, and he said he'd talk to his grandpa.

Today, I visited Dr. Daniels in his office, and I asked him why girls who have been abused will go out with a new guy who's abusive, or put up with an abusive guy. He said he didn't know. And I thought people went to a university to get answers. Then Dr. Daniels said it could be a combination of things, and it's always different for every person.

It could be self-esteem issues, it could be fear of the unknown. It could be all kinds of things. Dr.

Daniels said his sister had an abusive boyfriend when she was in high school, and her staying with him was a self-esteem issue even though she had two loving parents. I guess there's not a cookie-cutter answer for everything.

That's given me some stuff to think about. That we might stay in what we know, no matter how unpleasant or abusive it can be, because we're afraid of the unknown. Because we're afraid of change. That bothers me because I know if other people can be that way, and I'm a person, I could end up like that and not realize it. Dr. Daniels said it can be manifested in ways like staying in bad relationships to combat loneliness, or staying in a career we hate, or refusing to leave a certain town for a new one. The list could go on and on.

But I know one thing. I don't ever want to keep doing something I know I shouldn't, just because it's comfortable.

I haven't seen Shannon in a while, but I think about her all the time. I miss her. And I think about that abusive boy David, and all the abusive men and women in the world, and wonder why Shannon can be so mad at me when my lies weren't targeted at her. I would never raise my voice or hit her. I wouldn't do anything to hurt her, not intentionally, anyway.

Last night, I took her ribbon from my desk drawer and laid it on my pillow beside me. I don't know why I do that sometimes. But when I do, it's like she's with me.

I saw Aiden today, talking with a group of friends by the fountain. And I didn't feel like he had any power over me anymore. So, I just dropped a stale-faced nod at him and kept walking. His face went grim and he looked away.

It's amazing how confessing something you're hiding can bring healing and peace and freedom, in such a short time.

BB

April 16, 2000

The craziest thing happened yesterday. Finn went to see Eden at her apartment and Joanna handed Finn a note that Eden had left him. It was a Dear John letter and Eden told Finn that she had to go back home to Colorado. She asked him not to hate her, but that if he ever loved or respected her, to not contact or try to find her. Man, what a way to go out.

Joanna found the note on the kitchen counter. All of Eden's stuff was moved out of the apartment that morning. Joanna said that last night Eden had been an emotional wreck, but wouldn't tell her what was wrong. She didn't think it had to do with Finn. Joanna called Ryan while we were in the caf and told him what happened.

Ryan and I ran to our apartment, and Finn had

just gotten back. He was holding the letter in his fist. The letter was all crunched up. He was furious. I've never seen him like that before. He asked us if we knew anything about it, and we didn't.

Finn yelled, "I don't want to hear Eden's name mentioned in this apartment again! Unless someone knows what happened to her." Then he stormed into his room, slammed the door, and I heard him throwing stuff around.

Later, Finn asked Joanna to find out what happened to Eden. Joanna called an information line, but Eden's family's name wasn't in the Colorado Springs phonebook. So Joanna called Pepperdine's administration to get Eden's home phone number, but they weren't allowed to give it out, or they didn't have it.

Joanna called City Hall in Colorado Springs, but they wouldn't give her Eden's family's number, either. Joanna and Ryan even visited her professors, but they didn't know what happened. She just disappeared. The staff in the housing department said Eden's dad signed her out, but that was the only clue.

Poor Finn. I can't imagine what that would be like. I think my problems are bad until I hear other people's problems. Finn said Eden had been weighed down by family issues lately, and she'd never tell Finn exactly what those issues were. He said she was a bit down and distracted yesterday, but nothing too alarming.

I mean, what causes someone to do something like that? What's so terrible in her life or in her family's life? And now Finn has to live without having any closure at all. I mean, as far as he knows, she's dead.

I'm afraid this experience will leave a scar on him, a scar that will remain with him for the rest of his life.

BB

April 22, 2000

Finn's grown distant. I see him less now, even less than I did when he and Eden were dating. He still works out in the mornings while I'm still in bed, and I'm already in bed again when he comes back in at night. It's crazy.

His room's really messy. His bed is never made. Clothes and papers are always strewn and scattered in all kinds of places. That's the only way I know he's even been here. Things are shifted around again, and that's it.

Yesterday, I saw him for the first time in a week. I was in Diedrich's, studying, and Finn walked in. "Finn!" I yelled, setting my book down and jogging over to him. He barely smiled at me. I could tell whatever smile he smiled was forced. His face was unshaven and his shoulders drooped. The light was gone from his eyes. "How are you?" I asked, shaking his hand. "I haven't seen you in a while."

Finn looked away and it was hard for him to look me in the eye. And he kept running his hands over his cheeks and across the back of his neck like he was going crazy or something. "Ah, fine," he muttered. "Just getting ready for finals." He cleared his throat and swallowed and then looked away. I mean, he had crazy depression in his eyes. He really did. It was spooky, like he was a completely different person.

"Is there anything I can do?" I asked.

"No," he said, and this time he maintained eye contact with me. "But thanks."

Then last night, around 9:30 p.m., I returned to the apartment, and the light in Finn's bedroom was on. His door was shut. Ryan was out. I emptied my pockets onto my dresser. I figured I'd check on him, so I started toward my door. But then I heard a loud thud against the wall and the sound of a book falling to the floor. And then Finn screamed something indecipherable and punched the wall twice. *Pow.* Half a second. *Pow* again.

I heard him busting up stuff in his room, like he was taking a baseball bat to everything. Then, Finn swung his door open and burst out in his sneakers and sweat pants with his sweatshirt in hand. He didn't even glance into my room. He just passed by and kept going, eyes forward. They were burning, red hot. I mean, it scared me.

I peeked into his room after he left, and it looked like an angry man had gone apey in his room. Finn had put his fist through the wall, and his crosse was bent and lying on the middle of the floor. Anything that once had a place in his room had been busted up or was torn apart. I mean, I think Finn's losing it.

I never heard Finn come back because I fell asleep. And when I woke this morning, he was gone again. But he had been there. All his books and papers were pushed aside to clear a path to his bed.

I saw Ryan later and I asked him about it, if he thought Finn would be all right, and if there was any news about Eden. Ryan said he doesn't know if they'll ever know what happened to her, or if Finn will ever get over it.

"Finn was in love with her," Ryan said, shaking his head. "He would have married her. But Finn doesn't say much about his personal life. If he wants to talk about it, he will."

I hope they find out what happened to Eden one day, and I hope Finn can be with her again. No good man who loves a woman that much should be separated from her, I don't think.

BB

April 25, 2000

I'm nineteen years old, and after growing up on the wrong side of the tracks, and then on the right side of the tracks, and having a job, and visiting the east coast, and living on the west coast, I thought I'd seen just about everything. But it's amazing how life has the tendency to always teach us stuff.

Back on Thursday, Ryan and I were having lunch in the caf. By the way, Finn met with Dr. Daniels and they had a long talk about Eden. Ryan doesn't know for sure what all they talked about, but Finn isn't irate like he was last week.

I don't think they found out what happened to Eden, though. I think it was a mentor-to-pupil talk, like Yoda to Luke Skywalker. But Ryan said Finn's still real quiet and Ryan catches Finn staring off into outer space when they're together.

So we were in the caf, and Tabs walked by, and I know she saw us. Because we all sit at the same table everyday, around the same time, and there's not that many people in the caf. But Tabs came in and she was whiter than usual, like she'd been staying inside all the time. Her eyes were red and puffy like she had been asleep all day.

Everyone has to buy their food at one of two cash registers that stand side by side, and the exit faces the dining room where we all sit. So Tabs made quite the effort to not look in our direction when she bought her food and left.

That bothered all of us. Ryan just shook his head. I wondered if he was going to say or do something, but he and Tabs have known each other for two years, and she and Finn are really close, and those guys seem to know when to step in and when to keep their distance. Ryan said Finn's tried talking to her all he can, telling her she deserves better and needs to get out of that abusive relationship. But it all falls on deaf ears.

Well, it all came to a head Friday night. Ryan and I were sitting in the living room talking after dinner and we were thinking about watching a movie. Suddenly Finn burst into the apartment. "Where's your car keys?" he yelled at Ryan, real panicky.

"Here," Ryan said, fishing them out of his pocket.

Finn told us Ethan was having a party, and that Tabs called the library from Ethan's house, asking for Finn. Finn got to the phone, because he was studying in the library, and all Tabs said was, "Finn, come get me," and hung up. We don't have a phone in our apartment. Finn thinks someone slipped something into her drink.

Music was blaring and that's all he heard. And she used this tone like she wasn't right in the head. If David, her boyfriend, is with her, then why was she roofied? Finn tried calling Ethan's house back, but all he got was the busy tone.

So the three of us jumped into Ryan's car, and Ryan drove because Finn wanted to hop out as soon as he could. We got to the house. Ryan has asthma and can't run, so he stayed with the car. But Finn and I ran into the house. I don't know how Finn knew where to go, but he headed straight upstairs to where all the bedrooms are.

David, who I saw for the first time that night, was drinking and laughing with two girls on the back deck. Just before Finn climbed the stairs, he saw David through the window, which meant Tabs was probably still at the party. Finn asked me to check the downstairs bathroom.

I didn't know where it was, so I zipped through the house real quick and found the bathroom beside the kitchen. The door was closed, and after I knocked on it a few times, and then banged on it, a girl I've never seen before opened it. She was holding lipstick and was obviously put off by my ruckus. So I jetted upstairs to join Finn.

I noticed that a pole on the handrail was loose and leaning against the other poles. Ethan had probably been playing swords again. Upstairs, all the bedroom doors were open and the lights were off, except one. Under the door, I could see a dim light.

Finn was banging on that door and yelling, "Who's in there? Let us in! It's an emergency." But we didn't hear anything. Finn twisted the knob and slammed his shoulder into it, but it didn't do any good. I drop-kicked it above the handle twice, but that didn't work.

A fire extinguisher hung on the wall down the hall, so I ran and grabbed it. Finn stood back, and with two hits above the handle, I busted the deadlock through the door frame. Inside the room there was Tabs lying on the bed with her jeans zipped but unbuttoned, and her shirt pushed up to her bra. Two frat boys who I've never met before were scurrying to straighten their clothes, wide-eyed, wondering who we were.

All frat boys dress the same, so you can see them from a mile away. Finn didn't spend any time looking around or scorning them. He just ran over to Tabs and checked on her. She was barely awake, definitely drugged, but she was all right. Finn was picking her up to cradle her and take her downstairs, and then everything went hazy for me, then kind of black. Like I had taken a nap or something.

Next thing I know, I'm standing downstairs in front of the front door and in my right hand I'm holding that handrail pole that Ethan plays swords with. The music is off, and everyone at the party is frozen and staring at me, including Finn. He was holding Tabs, and he yelled, "What's wrong with you?!" which is what brought me back, I guess.

I looked at the glass front door, where we would be exiting, and its frame was there but the glass was completely broken out. And there was this guy with blood all over his face, lying on the front porch, coughing, and a guy and girl our age were sitting on their heels in front of him, making sure he was all right and looking back at me like I was a lunatic.

My right elbow was stinging, and I looked at it, and there was blood on it. "Get in the car!" Finn screamed at me, and out we went. And I'm not sure why, maybe to protect myself, but I took that pole with me. Ryan was already opening the back car door for us, and Finn slid Tabs in.

Finn took the wheel and made Ryan sit in the passenger seat. And while Finn drove, he looked back at me and had this look on his face like I was bat you-know-what crazy. "You didn't have to do that!" he yelled. And I was afraid to ask him what all happened because I couldn't remember, and I didn't want to come off as being even crazier than I looked. Later, I was able to remember some of it, and Ryan filled me in on the rest.

I caught up with those two frat boys from the bedroom, and I'm pretty sure I punched the first one in the chin and flipped him onto his back and then busted the other one in the eye. And when we got downstairs, some other guy jumped in front of us to block the door. I think he was afraid of getting in trouble if we took Tabs to the hospital and the cops showed up. But I grabbed the pole and hit him in the chest with it, and when he fell forward, I busted his nose with my elbow. Then I kicked him and he fell back and through the glass door. It wasn't a thick glass door. It was real flimsy.

I actually don't regret what I did one bit. I'm just sorry I freaked Finn out and ruined Ethan's door. When Ethan's parents come home, he definitely won't be able to hide that party. We took Tabs to her dorm and reported the incident to the resident assistant. She was a junior, and she looked after Tabs.

The two frat boys who were alone with Tabs weren't from Pepperdine. But they were members of David's fraternity, just a different chapter. They were visiting from some tech university I've never heard of before.

The day after the party, Finn found David's apartment off campus and visited him. Finn said he was diplomatic with David and told him he needed to stay away from Tabs, or Finn would make some calls and have David kicked out of his fraternity, and maybe even Pepperdine. According to Finn, David didn't say much. He just nodded and said he was sorry, and that was the end of it.

Tabs is doing much better. Finn and Ryan and I ate lunch with her today in the caf and she said she had a headache the day after it happened. She didn't remember Finn and me busting into the room or taking her back to the dorm, but she remembered calling Finn at the library. She thanked us for coming to get her. She didn't mention David's nose, but I know she knows. I guess some things are better not brought up again, and we can just leave the past alone.

Through all of this, I've seen Finn become more

himself again. Maybe it's because everything that happened with Tabs was a distraction, or maybe it was because he was helping someone and not dwelling on his own personal losses. He's still going to the gym and playing lacrosse, and I think that helps a lot, but I think helping Tabs brought the most healing to him. Psychology is an amazing thing. It really is.

Today, Shannon found me in the caf and hugged me and said she heard about what happened. Ryan told her. She said Ryan told her I busted a door down and beat up two guys to save Tabs' life. Well, that's a bit of an exaggeration, but Shannon was looking at me like I was some kind of hero, and I wasn't going to throw that away.

So I just said, "Tabs wasn't about to die, but she was in danger. And I didn't beat the guys up. I just hit them to get them out of our way." Shannon believed I was being modest. But you know what? I was being honest. And that felt good. I'm growing, I guess.

After that, Shannon and I rode to Diedrich's and I bought a coffee and bought her a tea, and I asked for her forgiveness about the accent and told her I was sorry. She said I was forgiven, but to never lie to her again. She said that she cares about me, but she can't be friends with people who lie to her. I told her I'd never lie to her again, and I mean it. Then, when I told her I was sorry again, she nodded and said it's in the past. But the fact that all is well between us now makes me really happy.

She told me about her time in Los Angeles when she came back after New York. She said she was getting small acting parts here and there. She was a maid in a soap opera, and even visited a modeling agency here. They called after seeing her headshots.

But when she walked in, the agency guy was shocked and said, "Oh no, you've put on some weight. You need to lose at least fifteen pounds and get your hair done." But Shannon was like, nah, and decided she likes the way she looks.

And I said, "Yeah, I always liked the way you looked." I didn't mean anything inappropriate by it, and I know she realized that, because she leaned back and laughed. I love her laugh. Man, I really do.

At one point in our conversation, she propped her chin in her hand, and a lock of her hair fell over her wrist, and I was reminded of that mirror image on the couch in New York. I had to look away and swallow hard, because she about killed me. I sipped my coffee to keep myself calm.

We spent the next half hour or so talking and laughing. I knew it couldn't last long because we had studying to do, more her than me, but I'm glad we hung out and talked. That hurdle is over, meaning that we are back together on good terms, and I feel really happy.

If we never date or get married, I'm all right with that, because I know I love her. And being friends is enough if it means I can keep loving her and just be in her presence.

That attitude's important.

BB

Chapter 4

May 1, 2000

Finals are in three weeks, and Finn called me while I was studying and asked if I wanted to go for a ride in Ryan's car. Ever since Finn helped rescue Tabs, he's been smiling more, but not like he was before he met Eden. He's not his full self yet, and I'm not sure he'll ever be.

I decided not to bring up the issue of Eden. I figured if he wanted to talk about it, like Ryan said, he would. So we went to Westward Beach and parked the car and went for a walk around sunset, right after the heat is gone, but just before it's too cold.

We saw three dolphins diving toward the sunset, and I thought that was really special. I'd never seen dolphins in real life before.

Finn listened to me mostly, wanting to know what it was like to grow up in Tuscaloosa, and what I did for fun back home.

I think it was just a comfort for him to have someone there to walk and talk with. He asked if I had any funny stories to tell. So, I told him a story about a guy I knew of in high school named Lee who graduated a few years before I did. And he had sex for the very first time in his parents' swimming pool, while they were away.

Word got out and during their senior night at the cafeteria, when all the seniors announced what they were leaving behind to the upcoming class, someone slipped this in: "And Lee would like everyone to have a copy of *The Little Mermaid*." All the students burst out laughing. Even Lee laughed about it.

I told another story our teacher told us in middle school. One Christmas when my teacher was a little girl, one of her older brothers got on the roof of their house and trampled on it so everyone could hear it inside. Then her other older brother said it was Santa Claus, grabbed a shot gun, and said he was going to blow Santa's head off. So he went outside and fired into the air and the brother on the roof started throwing wrapped gifts to the ground. Our teacher said she cried and cried.

Finn said he had a friend named Chelsea, and when she was seventeen, she and her family were at a theme park. Chelsea saw a little boy in a security guard uniform, walking with his dad, also dressed in a security guard uniform.

Chelsea thought it was adorable and she bent over and rested her hands on her knees and said to the little boy, "Oh my gosh! You are so cute! Are you dressed like your daddy today?" Chelsea was thinking it might be a Father-Son Day or something. But the kid gave her this real hateful look, and when she zeroed in on his face, she realized he wasn't a boy, but a midget.

Finn was laughing by that time, and it was good to finally hear it. But it didn't last long. Because after the jokes passed, he got quiet again. I really hope things turn out well for him. And I hope he knows that he can always be himself with me. He doesn't have to act a certain way, or wear a mask, or use filters in what he says.

I think that's what makes a true friend. When you can be your complete self, and the other person likes you and would be there for you through anything.

BB

May 7, 2000

Today I walked into Finn's room, and he was packing his suitcases. He's let his beard fill in and he looks like a mountain man.

On his floor and bed were three boxes for books, two suitcases filled and zipped, and a handful of clothes on their hangers lying across his bed.

"You're leaving?" I asked.

"Yeah."

"School's not finished yet," I said. There's still another week before finals.

"I talked to my professors. I took my exams and passed my Master Comps. They're letting me leave early."

"Where you going?"

"Africa. I got the call a few weeks ago. They need help with street kids and micro-lending, so I'm going."

"Who?"

"A place in Nairobi called Made In The Streets. They work with street kids, so I'm going to help." He was barely looking at me. As if he was pretending to be too focused on packing. But everything was already packed, for the most part. He was just fidgeting. I'm afraid he's losing it! And I thought I was screwed up.

"When are we going to see you again?" I asked.

"I don't know. But you'll see me again," he said. And then he stopped, looked at me, and said something really nice that he didn't want me to miss. "I don't forget my friends."

"Will you ever come back to Pepperdine?"

"I'll never leave Pepperdine, Oz. I might live in other places. But I'll never forget this place. I'll always come back."

"Will you write? And let us know how you're doing?"

"I will if I can. Have you talked to Dr. Daniels?"

"Not yet. I'm still working up the courage. Aiden has let up, so that's been good."

"I wouldn't waste any more time," Finn said. "It'll be much better on you if you confess to Pepperdine first, before Aiden or someone figures it out."

"When are you leaving?"

"Tonight." Finn was planning to stop by his home in Tennessee to see his grandpa on his way to Africa.

So, Ryan and I drove to Ralphs Grocery Store and bought some steaks, and we cooked them for us and Finn as a going-away gift. Over dinner, I thought we'd have deep things to say and talk a lot, like we were catching up on future conversations that haven't happened yet. But we didn't. It was all just small talk. We were shocked, I guess. But Finn wasn't. It was like he had already left.

Finn, the joyous, happy-go-lucky guy I met and grew to care about at Pepperdine has turned into a sad, melancholic recluse in a matter of weeks. It's like a part of him has aged ten years. I noticed lines in his forehead and gray hairs on the side of his head that I've never noticed before.

Ryan and I said goodbye to Finn at the sidewalk outside our apartment as he boarded a shuttle to LAX. But at that last moment, right before he stepped onto the shuttle, I chased him down. I told him thank you for everything. I really didn't have any words other than that. And he smiled at me and said, "You're welcome." I think he under-stood. I really do.

I turned to leave and Finn yelled back, "Oz!" I spun around, and he said, "If something happens to me in Africa, I want you to do me a favor." I didn't want him to say stuff like that, but I nodded. He said, "If Eden ever comes back, or if you ever see her in the future, will you do something for me?" I nodded. "Tell her I love her. I really did love her. And for whatever reason she left, tell her I understand, and that I forgive her. Will you tell her, Oz? Please."

"I'll tell her," I said. And then Finn hugged me and said, "You're a good friend, Oz." And then he left.

I'm in my room now, and it's real quiet. Ryan's asleep. Finn's room is empty, and this apartment already feels colder and lonelier.

BB

May 9, 2000

Two days ago, Shannon found out that Will was cheating on her while he was on the road with his band. Multiple girls in multiple cities. One of the band members knew the whole time, was friends with Shannon, and made Will tell her. Shannon was devastated.

I hate that that happened to her, but I don't hate that she broke up with him. Because now Shannon and I might be able to be together. But I'm not going to push for us to have some one-on-one time. She needs to heal, I think.

Last night, I called up Ryan, Joanna, Tabs, Matt, and Patrick, and we all made Shannon go with us to The Beanery. Shannon was sad at times, but happy at other times when we made jokes, and I'm glad she was smiling. Matt and Patrick used their gift cards and bought me supper. I ate pancakes. That might have destroyed my waistline, but I don't care right now.

I'm no longer speaking with the Irish accent and Matt said he could tell my accent was waning after having lived in California for a year. Ryan and Shannon just smiled.

Later, we went to Diedrich's for iced coffees and everyone got their favorite syrups put in, but I bought hot tea with milk and honey in Finn's honor. Then, we all went for a walk on the beach.

The moon was shining and the air felt really nice. It was cool but not biting. I was glad to be with all my friends, and I was glad Shannon was there with us. We didn't hold hands and she didn't loop her arm through mine. We all just walked and talked, and that was fine for us. It's nice to feel like I belong somewhere.

I looked back once, and I saw her and Tabs and Joanna walking and laughing together. And then I looked over at Ryan, Matt, and Patrick, and they were talking about a road trip up to Oregon that they want us all to take together one day. I felt at peace and I realized if it weren't for me, our little group wouldn't have formed.

I've been thinking about the upcoming summer,

what I'll do. Ryan will be working in the admissions department and staying in the apartment. He said I could stay there, too, and even crash on his floor if we have three more students assigned to our apartment. Shannon will graduate with her MFA, but she's thinking of sticking around to teach. I hope she does! If not, then maybe she'll teach at a school close by. There are plenty of schools in L.A.

Coogie's, the restaurant next to Diedrich's, is hiring for the summer. And I'm thinking of putting in an application. It's a lot like The Beanery because they serve everything from steaks to pancakes, but it's a bit more sophisticated, not as many beer choices, and it closes at 10 p.m.

I know I'll have to come clean with Uncle Mike and Aunt Karen when the time's right. I'm not a quitter, so even if I'm kicked out of Pepperdine, I can go to school at Santa Monica College and work at Coogie's, and still be close to Shannon and everyone else. That is, if Shannon stays close by. I can apply to Pepperdine the following year.

If Shannon teaches at a different college, I might go where she goes and get a job and attend school there. I'll ask her about that when the time's right. I don't want to smother her.

I feel good about the future, no matter the outcome. I really do.

BB

• • •

May 13, 2000

Finals are nearing. I haven't seen Aiden around much, and I'm glad. I've decided to finish out the semester, end my freshman year, and then go see Dr. Daniels about what I've done and see if he has any advice for me.

It looks like I'll have another A, mostly B's, and a C+ in math. That's better than the C- I had last semester. I'm not going to complain about that. I had to use a tutor the entire time, but I'm kind of proud of myself because Pepperdine's a prestigious school and I've done well.

I called Shannon yesterday and asked her to have dinner with me. I thought it was okay, and I was right, because she said yes. So I borrowed Ryan's car. I told him I'd put a full tank of gas in it for him, but he said it wasn't necessary. But I did anyway.

I picked Shannon up at her apartment, and opened all the doors for her. She always smiled and said thank you, and it took me back to that night on the boat, when I opened the doors for her and draped my jacket across her shoulders and held her from behind as we watched the Statue of Liberty.

We went to Duke's, a restaurant that overlooks the beach in Malibu and closes at 9 p.m. The restaurant was mostly empty, and we just talked about what was going on in our lives, how her job as a waitress was going, her studies, the few girlfriends she had. She ordered two girly drinks but I didn't order a drink because I'm not twenty-one.

I told her about how I've witnessed so many stories at Pepperdine that could be made into movies or novels, if someone just took the time to write them. Shannon said that with all of my journal writing, I should write a book about it all. I hope Finn finds Eden one day and they figure out what happened.

After dinner, Shannon and I went for a walk in Alumni Park. During the day, students play there, studying and throwing frisbees. But at night, no one ever hangs out there. It's because there's not a beautiful view of the city. It's just dark, but wide open, kind of like being on a golf course at night.

Shannon and I walked beneath the coral trees, their limbs like liquid silver against the moon. We could hear the waves crashing in the distance. Shannon slipped her arm into mine. And that felt good. Her skin and hair were beautiful, and she was glowing like an angel.

I could smell the sweet liquor on her breath. I paid for dinner, but she refused to let me pay for her drinks. I don't know why, but I really love the smell of liquor on her breath. I've never smelled liquor on a girl's breath before, but there's something about it that drives me crazy in a good way. I think it's because it tells me she has a naughty side.

She said she appreciated how sweet and kind I was to her, and that I hadn't tried to rush things. It was the first time either of us had spoken that openly about us. It's amazing how two people won't address the elephant in the room, and then sometime later, they'll bring up the issue as if it's been out in the open the entire time. But if you had spoken about it any earlier, the other person might have run for cover and stopped hanging out with you completely. Relationships are strange. The things we do in relationships don't make a lot of sense sometimes.

All I could think to answer was, "You're welcome." And at that, she stopped, and with her soft grip on my arm, she turned me around. And she didn't try to kiss me or give me the look that she wanted me to kiss her. Instead, she just wrapped her arms around my neck and hugged me, and I hugged her, too.

We must've stood like that for twenty minutes or so. I rubbed her back and she inhaled real deep and let out a soft moan. That about drove me crazy, but I didn't let on.

Sometimes silence can deliver more messages than words, and that moment with her was really beautiful. She's a hugger, for sure. She loves to hug. And I don't mind.

After I drove her back to her apartment, we

hugged each other in the car again, and I couldn't help but wonder if I would ever be the kind of man she needed. And if she decided to marry me, would she later realize I wasn't the man she wanted, and then regret it. I know it's dumb to think of those questions right now, but I can't help it.

I have so many thoughts. I'm all over the place. Sometimes I think I'm crazy. I really do.

BB

May 15, 2000

Today couldn't have been a better day. Matt, Patrick, Tabs, Joanna, Ryan, Shannon and I began dead week where we're all studying for finals. But none of us have any pressing exams to study for, so we went to The Beanery one last time, because we all know we won't hang out again until next fall.

I made a gift for everyone. I wrote each of them a personal letter and listed what I liked and admired about them. Each letter was hand-written on art paper with the sides ripped off, and I put that drop of hot red faux wax below my signature and stamped it. I had ordered a kit after I used Finn's.

For Matt and Patrick, I thanked them for taking me into their circle when they didn't know me, and always wanting to hang out and have fun without having to know every single thing about my life. I told Tabs I thought she was real courageous, because she had the courage to pick herself up again after that abusive boy in high school. How she came to college halfway across the country to start all over again. And then to have the courage to walk away from David, too, and start all over again, again.

I wrote a short letter to Joanna, apologizing for not spending a lot of time with her, but saying that I knew she was a great girl if Ryan was dating her. I also said that if I ever become the kind of man Ryan is, I'd be happy. Joanna showed that part to Ryan and he smiled. And to Ryan, I wrote two pages, thanking him and Finn for opening their apartment to me when they didn't know me, and for not judging me about Ireland. I also wrote that I admired his integrity. That the Ryan everyone sees in public is the same Ryan in his apartment, in private, when no one's looking. He liked that, too.

I thought about writing a letter to Finn and getting his address from his grandpa, but if I was going to tell Finn how much I loved and respected him, I'd want to give it to him in person and have him read it in front of me, so that we could talk about it. So I'm not going to.

I wrote Shannon a simple paragraph. I said, "I'm really thankful we met in New York and that we met again in California. You've made a huge difference in my life. And I want to spend our friendship showing you my gratitude, rather than just writing about it in a letter." And that was it. Not very romantic, I know. But I meant every word.

I actually drafted a longer letter to Shannon, but I decided not to give it to her. I just needed to get it out of my system. Here's what I wrote:

Dear Shannon,

You're my first love, and my only love. There are times when I would've given anything to hold you again and run my fingers through your hair, and listen to you talk about your day, but I couldn't because of Will.

I hope you know that when you're happy, or sad, or joyful, when you're melancholy on spring days, or rainy nights, or autumn evenings, I'd be right there with you, watching the leaves change. And during cold winters by the popping and cracking of a chimney fire, as the snow powders the limbs of the cedars, I'd be there with you, lying beside you when you wake up and when you go to sleep.

And I'd never abandon you. I'd be there for you when you need me. And starting now, I'll be there for you as long as my time on earth shall last. All you ever have

to do is tell me what you want or need and I'll provide that for you if it's within my power. I swear I'll love you the rest of my life.
—Brian

But I can't give that to her. She'd think I'm crazy. I think it's sad that you can't be completely transparent with the people you love. There has to be some sort of censorship. It's a way of protecting them.

Over dinner and drinks, we laughed and talked about stuff that happened over the year. Ryan recounted the story of how he and Finn found me sleeping in the library, thinking I had been kicked out of my room over sex. Tabs remembered meeting me for the first time and hearing me speak with my Irish accent. She said she thought it was hot. Tabs still doesn't know that I'm not from Ireland. Oh well. The truth will come out eventually.

I'm sure Joanna knows because she bites back a smile when the subject comes up. Matt and Patrick remembered how we would go to parties last semester, drink a lot, I would sleep on their couch, and then we would go eat pancakes in the caf. Tabs told the story of the frat party, rehashing what Finn and Ryan told her. Matt and Patrick said Ethan and other people at the party still talk about that night. They didn't have a clue what was going on. I never heard what happened about the door, if Ethan got in trouble or not.

Shannon told them our story, and she made it sound like I was visiting New York from Ireland, on account of Tabs, Matt, and Patrick. Tabs, being a girl, wanted the details of the love story. But Shannon looked at me to tell it.

"I caught Shannon looking at me outside the Hard Rock Café," I said. Shannon laughed, and Joanna smiled an I-know-that-girl-move smile. "I didn't mind," I continued. "I looked right back at her. And when she and her group walked past us, I smiled and waved. And of all the hotels in the entire city, guess which one she was staying in?"

"No way!" Tabs shouted. "That's amazing!"

Joanna nodded, and Shannon did, too. Then everyone was quiet, waiting to hear the rest.

"So we met up later that night in the lobby, and we took it from there."

"Tell me something else about you two," Tabs said, sipping her beer and peeking over its top at us. Even Matt and Patrick had leaned in at that point, wanting to hear the rest.

"Shannon?" I asked, looking to her for help.

"I remember how sweet he was," Shannon said. "We talked all night in his hotel room, lying on his bed. He listened and acted more mature than any boy I'd ever met. He was the perfect gentleman."

"Uh-oh," Tabs said, winking at me.

"He really cared," Shannon went on, her eyes

lingering on mine. That made me feel real good.

"It sounds like it was meant to be," Tabs said, and everyone smiled.

Matt held his iced tea up for a group toast, Patrick quickly followed, and then we all clinked our glasses together. Matt said, "To Brian and Shannon." Then, everyone said it in unison.

"Wait," I said. And everyone paused. "To us all," I finished. Shannon laid her head on my shoulder and I could feel her smile. I smelled the vanilla in her hair, and I about died again. It was a beautiful moment, and I didn't want the night to end.

Eventually people trickled out until it was just Shannon, Tabs, and me. We walked Tabs to her car and hugged her goodbye. I asked Shannon if she wanted to go home and she said no. So we came back to my apartment.

In my bedroom, the moon made the walls glow. I popped into Ryan's room, since he wasn't there, and borrowed his boom box and Eagles CD. Shannon and I listened to songs like "Tequila Sunrise", "I Can't Tell You Why", and "New Kid In Town" while we lay on my bed and whispered. At first she laid her head beside mine, on my pillow. But before long, her head was on my chest, and I was raking my fingers through her hair.

She asked me what my first year in California was like, coming from Alabama. And all I could think to say was, "It's amazing how much can change in just one year."

"Or just a few months," she added, and smiled at me, blinking softly. Her eyes held mine, and a smile broke out across her face. I felt my heart in my throat. And I couldn't stop thinking about how good she smelled.

"What?" she asked, her voice softer now.

"You're just like I remember in New York," I said.

"Is that a good thing?"

"Yeah. That night we had in New York, when we were talking on my bed, that was a really good night. And walking around the city, too. I'd never done anything like that before."

"But then you went on to do some great things."

"Like what?" I said.

"Well, like coming here for school. Do you know what you'll study?"

"It's still psychology. Later, I want to get my master's so I can get a counseling license."

"Why?" she asked.

"Because I want to help people."

"I remember you saying that in New York. It's admirable. You seem strong like that," she said.

"What do you mean?"

"You have an inner strength. When you want something, you really go after it. It's like you won't take no for an answer. I admire that about you."

I was stunned that she said that. I didn't really know that about myself until she pointed it out. But those were the same traits I admired in her. It made me feel good to hear that she saw traits like that in me.

"I have issues, though," I said before I could stop myself.

"We all have issues, Brian," she said. "All kinds of things happen to us. It's how we respond that matters."

I wanted her to know what I admired about her, so I lit her up with compliments. "You said I was strong." I started. "But Shannon, you are too. Both of us came here alone right out of high school. And look at all you've done. When things didn't work out the way you hoped, you had the courage to change direction, to start over, no matter what people said. And when you were offered that modeling job and turned it down after that agent said what he said, I think that shows a lot about you. It's not about winning for you. It's important to you to try to do what you want in life. Even if it doesn't work out the way you hoped."

Shannon smirked and said, "Yeah, but here I am, working as a waitress, and just now finishing school."

"Yeah, with an MFA. That's a terminal degree. You can be a professor and get paid as much as the Ph.D.'s. Right? So what's wrong with that?" I asked.

"Nothing."

"You're right, it's nothing. You should be proud of yourself. That's what you want to do right now, isn't it? At this time in your life? If acting doesn't work out, you can teach. If teaching doesn't work out, you can act. Or you can do both."

"I know," she said, but she still had that disappointment in her tone.

"One of the things I've been learning lately," I said, "is that we can't compare our lives to other people's lives. I'm sure girls your age are getting married and having kids. And I know that's what you want, too. But you're just twenty-three. And you finished your MFA in a year. Lots of girls these days are waiting until they're in their late twenties and even their thirties to get married.

"Life isn't a destination but a journey. That's what all the philosophers we read in class say, and I understand that. I mean, if life was a destination, well, what's the destination? If we think of it as a destination, we get anxious and mad when things don't work out. But if we see life as a journey, which is what it really is, we're more open, and we're more able to enjoy it. Because we're not entitled."

"Wow, Brian," she said. "You talk like one of those philosophers." Then she laughed. I looked away. I didn't talk like that, not before Pepperdine at least. "Sounds like college is making a difference in your life, too," she said.

"It is," I answered. "I love this place. I really do."

"I know," she said. Then she yawned and covered her mouth with her hand.

A fast song came on, so I leaned over and hit the next button. When I returned, our eyes locked. I took her hips in my hands and gently pulled her to me, and my nose touched the side of her cheek. I breathed in the scent of her and felt my heart speed up. I felt her breath on my neck, and I kissed her temple, then just below her ear. She drew a sharp breath. She took my hand and placed it on her cheek, pressed her forehead against mine, and closed her eyes.

We didn't say much after that. She just kept her eyes closed. I had forgotten how soft her skin felt, how natural and real and true it feels to touch her. We didn't kiss. If she wanted to, we would have. I just know it. I can read her sometimes. Her body language. So I didn't kiss her.

I must have dozed off, because a few minutes later she woke me when she shifted her head, which was still lying on my chest. I rubbed her back and ran my fingers through her hair again.

We were both quiet for a while. "What are you thinking?" she asked. Her tone was gentle and affectionate. I shook my head, not wanting to say any more, because I liked the silence with her. But she was waiting for a response.

"I was thinking about the last time I've spoken this openly."

"When?"

"When I was with you in New York, when we were in the hotel room. I'll never forget that night. It was one of the most amazing nights of my life. I had never met someone like you. I had never connected with anyone like that. Where I was just honest about everything. And I cared about you. I would've done anything you asked."

"And that's a good thing?" she asked, with a teasing smile. I knew she didn't need an answer.

"Yes. Honesty, openness, affection. That's what a woman wants, isn't it?"

She chuckled. "It sounds like you read that in a book."

"I did."

She laughed harder this time. "What was I like in New York?" she asked.

"Passionate, and very wise," I said.

"How so?"

"You were lying in my arms, and we were talking. And you said you understood the importance of focusing on the good in people, drawing that out of them, like a finely-tuned radar system. I never forgot that. Tuned into the true, the good, the beautiful in others. Helping them see the good in themselves that they can't see. Uncle Mike said things like that, but I only heard things like that from him."

"Okay. I don't remember that, but it sounds good," she said, chuckling again.

"And I've learned since that it takes a lot of maturity to think like that. To see that people have traveled their own roads that we can't understand. Because we weren't there. We weren't with them. So it's hard to judge them. Actually, it's impossible to judge them. I think I really understood that when I met Tabs. When I heard about what happened to her and why she acted the way she did.

"In Dr. Daniels' class, we read this author named Norman Maclean. He wrote *A River Runs Through It*. And he said we can't fully understand our loved ones, but we can still love them completely. And now I ask myself, do I have the maturity to accept others? To accept their faults? Can I be all right with my own past and the fact that my life hasn't turned out like I imagined as a kid? Can I be all right with being human?"

After a long pause, Shannon said, "I'm sorry I wasn't friendlier to you when you came here. I'm sorry I didn't spend more time with you."

"Hey," I said, pulling out from under her and facing her across the pillow. "It's all right," I said. "I understand. I didn't know about Will, but when I did, I understood. And the stuff with your mom, and you didn't know I was coming to Pepperdine. It's okay. A lot of that is my fault. Besides, after it all happened, I came to a place where I was okay with just being friends with you."

"Really?" she said, lifting her head.

"Yeah. I care about you a lot. And if we're just friends, I can live with that."

And then, Shannon started to cry. She wiped her eyes two or three times. "I'm sorry," she whispered, and sniffled.

"No," I answered, sitting up. Then she sat up too.

"It's just that . . ." she tried to tell me, but then she couldn't. She burst into a sob, almost uncontrollably. She fell limp into my arms. And I leaned my back against the headboard and I just held her.

"It's all right," I whispered again. And after that, I stayed quiet until she was ready to talk. She leaned her head against my shoulder, sandwiched my hand between hers, and then she told me everything.

"It means so much to me that you're here," she said. "Because we met before it all happened." She swiped remaining tears from her face. "I'm sorry. Your shirt," she said, pointing to the mascara that splotched my shirt.

"I don't care about that."

"I know you care about me, and I knew I could trust you. There's more that I never told you. During the late spring, just after we met in New York, my apartment was broken into in West Hollywood. By the time I moved out, it had been broken into three times. Someone pickpocketed me when I was out one night, and I lost all my credit cards and all the money I had made in tips that week. After I called Mom and she wired some money, some friends and I went out that night, and I left my backpack with the money in the backseat of my friend's car. When we returned, the back window was broken, and my backpack was gone. None of the other cars had been touched.

"I moved out of that apartment. And I moved to Santa Monica, closer to work and school. Then Mom had her stroke. I know all that sounds impossible to have happened within a few months, but it happened to me. You know how one day you wake up and you realize the world isn't what you thought it was? That it's not safe? That you had just been blind and naïve to it the entire time? Nor Cal was so comforting and simple. I missed being a kid there a lot.

"When Mom had a stroke, I flew back home. I was almost fed up with being away. I spent a lot of time with my family and helped Mom regain the use of that side of her body. I met my family at the hospital. And I'll never forget the way Mom looked when I saw her. The side of her face just drooping. It scared me to see her suffering like that. I wondered why God let her suffer like that. Why not just take her out?" She gripped her temple with her hand and started crying again.

I didn't try to respond to that question. I've

learned that when people are hurting, they need a comforter, not a commentator.

"I had no idea," I said.

Shannon stroked my cheek. She wasn't looking into my eyes, but I felt her breath on my lips and her scent took control of me. I wanted her more than any woman I could ever imagine wanting. I wanted to kiss every inch of her skin and make love to her, and if my thoughts had been advertised to her, or anyone else in the world, I wouldn't have cared, as long as it meant us being together.

"I didn't think I'd ever see you again," she whispered.

"I knew I'd see you."

"How did you know?"

"I just knew. I was going to make sure of it," I said. Then I recounted to her how I hovered over her in the hotel room while she told me about her mom.

"Do you remember what I said?" Shannon asked.

"You gave the impression that your mom was going through a mid-life crisis, that she wasn't happy, and that if she could live her life over, she would've made other choices." Tears rolled out of her eyes again. She sniffed and wiped them away. And I continued, "I was hovering over you and listening. And you looked at me and said, 'You act as if you really care.' And I was shocked and hurt because I did care, and I said to you, 'I do care.'"

When I focused on Shannon again, her face was shining. I knew then that I was never going to let anything get in the way of loving her and one day marrying her. All I wanted was to tell her that I loved every memory of her, every facet, the way she talked, the way she laughed, how she was always kind to strangers, and if I could have one wish, that wish would be to spend the rest of my life with her.

Loving her would be my destiny. I knew that, even if I knew my love would never be returned. I wasn't afraid of love anymore. I wasn't afraid of her. Because I knew the love I had for her was real. We were real. And I was going to hang onto her with all my might.

"You know," she said. "It's interesting. Even back then, Mom was going through so much. I've worried about her for years. And after only knowing you for two days in New York, I confided in you about it all. You must have left quite an impression on me. You know what?"

"What?"

"You're the first person I've ever told that entire story to. Isn't it interesting how you can know someone for twenty years and not connect with them? But there are others you may have only known for a few months, and they'd put their life on the line for you. You'd swear you'd known them all your life."

"Yeah. I know what that's like," I said. I felt that

way about Uncle Mike and Aunt Karen. I felt that way about Finn and Ryan. And I felt that way about Shannon.

"You're like that," she said, looking up at me. And I leaned down, and we finally kissed, her mouth welcoming mine. We paused at various intervals, and continued those kisses until daybreak. I never tried to take her clothes off, and she didn't try to take off mine, even though I would have let her. Eventually, she laid her head on my chest again and we fell asleep, together.

Shannon has taught me that a man should know when to listen, when to talk, when to simply hold the woman he loves, and when to kiss her until her hurts go away. I'm trying to find the words to describe what being in love is like. It's like Shannon is every song I've ever heard, and every song that hasn't been composed. I feel like she's the embodiment of the invisible woman in all my dreams, the woman I've been purposefully created and fashioned for.

This morning, I walked her to her car, opened the door for her, and we kissed as the sunbeams burst forth behind us. It was awesome. When I returned to my bedroom, the scent of her hair remained on my pillow. And it felt like she was there with me as I drifted off to sleep again.

Being in love is wonderful. It really is.

BB

• • •

June 9, 2000

It's been three weeks, and I've waited until I knew I'd have some time to write, because I want to record this story in detail.

Sometimes we know when we're living in a moment that we'll remember for the rest of our lives. And when that happens, we wish we had it on video or written in detail. So, here goes.

The morning after Shannon left, I got a call around 6a.m. from Uncle Mike. That means 8 a.m. in Alabama, and Uncle Mike never calls that early because he knows I'm two hours behind. But he told me Mom died. He asked my input on the funeral arrangements, and I told him I didn't care. He thought it would be a good idea for me to come home, but I disagreed. He said I needed closure, and I said he was wrong.

It's the only time I've ever disagreed with him. I told Shannon about it, without sharing how sorry of a woman Mom was, but Shannon thought it was important I go.

I haven't seen Mom in years, but it doesn't bother me. I outgrew her a long time ago. Uncle Mike said that just because someone is family doesn't mean you have to be their friend or like them. Sometimes, there are friends who are closer than family. And we make our friends our family.

I remember Darren's funeral. I was eight years

old and crying, and Grandmother's brother, Leroy, pulled me aside. He lived three hours away. We had met once, a long time ago, at a family reunion. But Leroy, I guess, thought he was important to me. And he bent down, rested his hands on his knees, and said, "Dry those eyes, young man. Big boys don't cry."

That's the most horrible advice you can give a kid. If we weren't supposed to cry, God wouldn't have given us tears to shed.

As months passed after Darren died, living in the trailer with Mom became intolerable. She stayed drunk, yelled all the time, and when I needed anything, like money for school, or when there wasn't enough food for supper, she reminded me about my need to go trick-or-treating. That was the night Darren died, and she blamed me for it.

Deep down, I always believed she wished Darren and I could trade places. She seemed to always like him more. Grandmother said that if I ever wanted to live with her, I was welcome. But I didn't want to be in her way. Grandmother seemed happy, and I believed I had been the cause of so much unhappiness.

I don't know why I wrote all that, but I just wanted to share it. I've changed a lot, and not seeing Mom anymore or caring so much about what she thinks of me is actually a nice place to be.

So, given Shannon's advice, I hit the ground

running in Alabama, and Mom's funeral was at Grandmother's church. The youth minister, Thomas Turner, was nice and helped us with all the funeral arrangements. He's a few years older than me. But I noticed he was distracted a lot that weekend. He seemed fine until he heard my name. Then his face went white. It wasn't until later that I found out why.

Uncle Mike asked five of the fighters to serve as pallbearers. At the funeral, Grandmother's pastor made some comments and led a prayer, and then we buried Mom. I didn't cry. In my mind, Mom died a long time ago.

After the burial, Thomas shook my hand and apologized for our loss. And when we left, I looked over my shoulder and he was still watching me. I wasn't home long when the doorbell rang. Aunt Karen was busy with laundry and cooking for the pallbearers, but she answered the door and called my name, saying I had a visitor. Then she went back to work. I don't know where Uncle Mike was.

I went to the door and a man in his late twenties stood there. Clean-shaven, with a small gut, probably because of too many evening meals. He wore an orange polo shirt. His hair was cut close on the sides, almost shaved, but a bit longer on the top. He was trendy, wearing crisp jeans and leather loafers. And his eyes were red and watery, and it was impossible for him to smile.

He just looked devastated, like he was about to burst into tears.

"My little brother, Thomas, saw you at church," he said. I don't remember the exact words exchanged, because it's all blurry, but he said his name was Paul and "I was just a kid" and "We were all kids" and "It was an accident." And I knew then that he was one of the three boys who killed my brother. The other two boys there that Halloween night got into bad trouble years later. Drugs and gang stuff. One of them was killed and the other's in prison.

Paul told me that about a week after Darren's death, Paul's dad pulled him aside and said it was time to talk. Paul's parents knew something was wrong because Paul wasn't eating or sleeping. Paul broke down and told them everything.

Then, all their parents got together. They knew that if they came forward and confessed their kids' role in the death, their kids' lives would be ruined. The other two families left town, but Paul's dad was a professor at the university, so they stayed. Paul's an engineer now. He threw himself into work after high school, doing all he could to forget it. "I have a wife and kids now," he said.

I wanted to tell him he didn't care about Darren or me at all. That all he cared about was confessing and getting it off his chest. That if he really cared, he would've told us a long time ago. To give us closure. But I stood on the front porch and listened to get the whole story out of him.

When my hands and knees shook, I hid my fists in my jeans and squeezed them, trying to make them stop. I came in and out of consciousness, as far as I can tell. I think Paul needed me to tell him I forgive him, but I didn't. I stepped back into the house before we said anything else.

By the time I entered my bedroom, my reaction was a lot different. I'm good at stepping back into the protective places of myself, hiding, rebuilding, reassessing, where no one and no one's opinions can harm me. I was already devising a plan. I felt the anger, the fear, the helplessness, and a plethora of everything in between. I don't even have names for all the feelings.

I lay down on my bed and I went into this dream, the deepest and most real dream you can have while you're still awake. Darren was three years older than me, and he was the kind of kid who just always knew what to do. He had an old soul.

Mom used drugs, but she preferred alcohol over anything. Different men came to our trailer, stayed the night, and left. When a man came over, I could hear him charming her in her bedroom, talking sweet to her, and making her laugh. Then, they'd shut the door and turn on loud music. No child is stupid enough not to know what was going on.

Some men would yell and hit her. But most never stayed long enough to be boyfriends. They came, got what they wanted, and she did, too. And I guess for her, that was attention, affection, and drugs and alcohol.

I never got the full story, because Grandmother didn't like to talk about it. But Mom married a guy right out of high school. He beat her and was killed by a train. After that, Mom took to drugs and spiraled downhill. Darren and I were the result of her boyfriends. We don't believe we shared the same father. And that was all right with Mom because she got more money from welfare.

Darren and I shared a room where we slept on flattened cardboard boxes. And when the boyfriends came over or when there was shouting in the streets and gunfire, I'd ask him if he was scared. And he'd say, "No, go back to sleep. Everything will be fine in the morning." And he was always right. It was always fine in the morning.

That Halloween, I was eight years old, and Darren was eleven. It was our first time trick-or-treating. Mom said she bought the costumes at Walmart, but we both knew they came from Grandmother and Goodwill. We didn't care where they came from. We were just tickled to have them.

Darren was Zorro, and I was Superman. The sleeves were barely long enough to cover our wrists. The pants were tight in the crotch, and the legs only reached halfway between our calves and ankles. So we wore thermal underwear that Grandmother gave us to keep our arms and legs warm. Darren wore a black scarf with the eyes cut out for his Zorro mask. And I wore a plastic Superman mask. I remember the elastic string on the back pinching and pulling my hair.

Mom got high that night on weed and couldn't take us.

"Mom," I called down the hall. Darren and I had left our bedroom and were headed for the kitchen. "We're ready."

"Do y'all really have to go?" she yelled from her room.

"Yes!" I yelled, scared that Halloween was about to be cancelled. Her bailing out was typical. Darren and I had been looking forward to this night for months.

"We don't have to go, Mom," Darren said, "if you don't feel good."

"Darren!" I snapped, stunned he'd say that.

Mom was dizzy as she stumbled through the hall from her room. She tried to light a cigarette, but she couldn't balance her arm. The end of the cigarette kept dodging the flame. Then she waved her hand, dismissing us. "You boys go on. I ain't gotta take you."

Darren turned my shoulders and nudged me to the door. "Come on," he said.

"I'm sorry," I told him when we were in the yard. "But that's just like her."

"I know. It's okay," he said. "We'll go, and we'll have a good time."

We carried plastic Walmart bags to hold all the candy, and we walked from our neighborhood to a nicer one about a mile away. In the nice neighborhoods, the grass was the same shade of green in all the yards and trimmed to the same length. That's because of the professional lawn care and mowing services.

Glowing candles in white paper bags were lit along everyone's driveways. All sorts of different candies and chocolates were being given out. Some families even left packs of sweets on the front porch because they couldn't be there.

Grape and strawberry sugars melted in our mouths. We unwrapped silver-foil covered chocolates and melted them on our tongues. We loved it because we never got to eat candy.

"Trick or treat!" we said when every door opened. Some of the hosts were dressed up in costumes, but others stayed in what Darren called, "civilian clothes." After each candy stop, we'd laugh and skip on to the next house. The dew set on the grass, wetting our shoes, and grass trimmings stuck to our toes.

My shoelace came untied, so I kneeled to tie it. "Hurry!" Darren yelled at me, stopping and waiting.

"I'm trying!" He waited until I finished and then I caught up with him. We jogged side by side in a rhythm, onto the next house. Kids and their parents passed by, and we all waved and congratulated each other on our costumes. Star Wars, Scooby Doo, He-Man. Girls dressed as witches, princesses, and in My Little Pony gear.

When our bags overflowed and people started turning off their porch lights, Darren and I headed home.

We passed through the neighborhood where the roofs of people's houses and trailers were falling in. There wasn't electricity in a lot of them, but people lived there anyway. Scrawny dogs walked alone and slouched with their heads hanging because they'd been kicked too many times.

The trip home was much quicker if we passed through hollows and yards. We knew the woods and trails well, and with the moonlight at our feet we found our way through the shortcuts, into a field, and then we eased onto the street that led home.

I remember the scuffing of our shoes against the sidewalks and the shifting of the candy in our bags. I remember Darren laughing at me when I said I hoped the candy wasn't licorice. He even agreed to trade some of my caramels for some of his chocolates. He liked caramels, even without any chocolate on them. I never understood that. How anyone can prefer caramel over chocolate astonished me.

Two blocks ahead, three kids who couldn't have been older than fifteen were walking our way.

Wearing hockey masks and carrying long walking sticks, the boys whacked at the overgrown grass sticking up through the sidewalks. They wore buzzed haircuts, white t-shirts, khaki cut-off shorts, hiking boots, and they carried old, large paint buckets to hold their candy. Their buckets swung and bobbed up and down, obviously empty. They must've just started, I thought.

When they grew close, I didn't think much of it, but Darren got quiet and placed his hand on my shoulder when the boys were just a few yards out. I knew that touch. I got quiet too. Darren always knew what to do in situations, so I followed his lead. If I had that night to live over again, I would have told Darren to drop the bags and sprint to the woods. But how was I supposed to know what would happen?

I remember hearing the boys talking and laughing and not paying us much mind, except the middle one. His eyes had watched us the entire time. When they passed, Darren said, "Happy Halloween," and the middle boy froze. His friends took a few more steps, but then they stopped, too.

"Come here," the boy said and then stepped toward us. Darren grabbed my arm and pulled me behind him. Darren took a step back when the boy looked into Darren's bag.

Then, like someone flipped a switch, he just snatched Darren's bag and dumped it into his bucket, laughing. I glanced at the other two boys. They looked at each other, shocked at what their friend had just done. Darren's hand moved toward the boy's bucket, but then he stopped. Darren decided against it, and let it go.

But then the boy reached for my bag, and Darren knocked his arm away. The boy pushed Darren back, and Darren stumbled over my foot, lost his balance, and fell to one knee, catching himself on the sidewalk with his right hand. When Darren fumbled to try to stand again, the boy raised his stick and brought it down, hard, striking Darren on the back of the neck. Darren fell over and he didn't move.

The boy grabbed my bag, began to walk away, but then stopped after two steps, and turned back to look at us. The other two boys hadn't moved at all. Now, all three were frozen, watching Darren. For a second or two, I thought Darren was playing dead.

"Hey," the lead boy said with some concern in his voice, stepping toward Darren. Then I think the reality of it all sunk into his head. Suddenly, he said, "Come on!" And the boys ran away.

I remember bending over, shaking Darren, begging him to get up. I sat down and pulled his head into my lap. His eyes were half open and his entire body was limp.

I heard children laugh in the distance and a dog bark. An adult ran up to us after hearing my cries. I don't know who he was. It's all a blur. The only part I'm thankful for that night is our laughter and the good times, and how Darren didn't suffer. According to the doctor, the stick broke Darren's neck and he had died instantly.

Many kids in those days dressed in white t-shirts and khaki cut-off shorts. Hockey masks were common during Halloween because *Friday the 13th* was popular. The three boys that day didn't have tattoos or piercings, and no names were said during the incident. So the police said identifying the boys would take time.

"The boys won't be able to keep it a secret," one cop said. They'd spill it to friends or girlfriends or relatives. They always did. Then people would come forth.

But that never happened.

Over time, that Halloween night fell into a legend. For years, parents accompanied their kids trick-or-treating. "Don't forget about what happened to that Bailey boy," they'd say. I hated hearing that. I wanted to shake them and tell them that his name was Darren, and he was my big brother, and he was the best friend a boy could ever have.

I never went trick-or-treating again. On Darren's birthday or Halloween every year, I'd go for long walks and hope tomorrow would come in a hurry.

As the years passed, bitterness and anger grew in me. I refused to return to that sidewalk where Darren was killed. And I swore if I ever found that boy who did it, I wouldn't use a gun or a knife. I'd just beat him to death with my fists.

I dreamed about Darren for years. I still do, every now and then, but the dreams aren't as frequent these days. In most dreams, we're playing at the Black Warrior River where Grandmother took us sometimes. A flash of light comes, as if changing scenes in a movie, and Darren's pulling me into a soft headlock, looking into my eyes, and saying, "I'm proud of you, little brother."

But other times, I dreamed about the boy in that hockey mask, raising his stick and coming down with it across Darren's neck. Darren's eyes go limp, and he starts kicking and peering up at me, as if pleading for my help. He coughs up blood and it runs out of his mouth and over his cheek. That's not how it happened, but those are the images in my dreams.

For years, I blamed myself. Couldn't I have just handed the candy to the three boys? Or pushed Darren out of the way? What if we had stayed home like Mom asked us? And what about those times Darren stopped and waited for me, like when I had to tie my shoes or wipe the dew-soaked grass off? Couldn't I have run faster to catch up? Or maybe I could have just kept Darren waiting a few more seconds. That way, the boys would have passed on by and we'd never have met them.

I woke from my daydream and shot off my bed. I jetted into the kitchen, and I skimmed the phone book for Turner. Five were listed in Tuscaloosa. But none were Paul. Uncle Mike and Aunt Karen were busy talking, discussing plans for supper. Tony and some of the other fighters, the pall-bearers, were on their way over.

I grabbed the cordless phone, stepped onto the back porch, and dialed the first number in the phone book. A middle-aged woman answered.

"Yes, is this Thomas and Paul's house?" I asked. I could hear my heart beating in my ears.

"No," she answered. "That's Gerald. Those are Gerald's boys." Gerald Turner was second on the list.

I hung up and dialed Gerald's number.

"Hello?" answered a weak, older woman's voice.

"Hi. My name's Jude. Is Paul there?"

"He doesn't live here anymore."

"Is this his mom?"

"Yes."

"I'm an old friend of Thomas and Paul's. I've been gone a few years. I'd like to see Paul. I looked in the phone book but I didn't see his number."

"It's under Leeman Turner. Paul's his middle name."

"Leeman Paul Turner?"

"Yes. Would you like his number?"

248

I didn't need it. And I didn't stay on the phone any longer. I just hung up. His address was at Arrowleaf Circle in Cottondale. I knew exactly where that was. Arrowleaf was one of those neighborhoods where all the grass was cut the same length, where people who make over $100,000 a year lived. When I was a kid, I used to skip rocks in a pond over there.

I grabbed my coat and slipped out the back. I hopped into Mike's truck and ran my hand under the driver's seat. I felt Tony's billy club, just as I had left it there, four years ago. It's a rubber hose with the bolt shoved into its end.

The adrenaline rushed through my veins. My heart was pounding, hard now, in my chest, ears, and neck. My right leg shook as I pressed it down on the pedal. I felt lightheaded, but I shook it away.

I had promised myself that if I ever discovered who Darren's killer was, I'd beat him to death. And that's exactly what I was planning to do. I'd bury the hose in Lurleen State Park.

What had I been working toward? Making money? That didn't mean anything to me anymore. Make money to have a wife? That's not going to work out as soon as Shannon finds out how crazy I am. And I don't really care about marrying anyone else.

In less than five minutes, it was like a sleeping, raging beast had awakened. I recognized him from my childhood, but he was older now. Like he had been hibernating and growing stronger over the years. To stifle him felt like I would be strangling myself. Setting him free was like I'd be setting myself free, for the first time.

Nothing was worth more to me now than killing Paul. Whatever punishment I faced, I didn't care. I considered it worth it. I mean, I didn't even care if the cops caught me. Perhaps it would send a message to all the bullies in town. "Better stop before your violent past returns for you."

I rode into the subdivision and pulled into Paul's driveway. The home was brick with navy blue shutters and two white columns at the front. A brick staircase with black iron rails led to the front door. A brand new SUV was parked in the driveway with an Auburn University Engineering sticker on the back windshield. A successful man, as he had said. I wanted to kill him even more now. Take it all away from him, like he had taken everything away from Darren and our family.

Wild onions were growing in everyone's yard. I didn't see anyone outside, anywhere. I grabbed the hose and slid it up the back of my shirt and pushed the handle into my hip pocket. I stepped out and strode past his SUV and heard the hot motor popping, cooling off. He had just gotten home.

I skipped up the steps, opened the glass door,

and knocked on a heavy, wooden one. The brass door handle was locked. Three seconds felt like thirty. All my senses were finely tuned, like their volume had been turned up. I heard the rattling of a chainsaw in a neighboring subdivision. A dog barked in a backyard several houses down.

I tried to drop all aggressive emotions from my face and stance, so I'd seem like I had come by for another chat. When Paul opened the door, aromas of banana-nut bread and cinnamon spilled onto the porch, and I heard a young woman's laughter behind a wall. I smiled at him, diplomatically. To the side of his arm, I saw a sun-yellow toy baseball bat on the living room rug. Paul watched me, curious as to what I was doing there. The glass door separated us. He cracked it open, but not any further.

I was thinking about clubbing his knees, and then hitting him across the neck while he was hunkered down. If he lunged after me, I'd side-step and bring the club down across his head. But, none of that can ever be planned. You have your plans, but they go out the window when the fight begins.

As soon as his hand pushed down the latch on the glass door, I swung the door open, caught his collar, and jerked him forward, making him stumble off balance. I grabbed the club, reared back, and hit him across the side of the face with it. I'm not sure why I chose not to hit his neck at that last second. I guess it's because I didn't really want to kill him. Not deep down, anyway. Paul fell to his knees, barely making a sound.

I dropped the hose and I started pounding his head with my fists and kneeing him in the face. Blood started draining from his nose and mouth, but I kept working on him. He never screamed and he never fought back. He didn't even retaliate except raising his hands up, trying to protect his face and head.

I feel horrible for all of this now. At the time, it was as if I had stepped outside myself and was watching everything. I was telling myself to stop, but I just kept on. And while I was hitting him, the unexpected happened. His lip started quivering and his jaw shook, and he just burst into tears. But it wasn't because of the beating. It was emotional.

Then I heard the cries of a kid from the house, and I stopped and looked up. My left hand had a fistful of Paul's collar, holding him up so I could pound on him. And this little boy, no older than six, shot out of the house and lay down on top of his dad, holding his hand up for me to stop.

And he was letting out this horrible, rattling cry. "Daddy! Daddy!" he screamed. And then, Paul tried to push his son out of the way, to make sure his son didn't get hurt. A pretty lady with a mother's shape ran to the door, and then she froze, looking at me and covering her heart with her hand.

I let go and moved as fast as I could off the porch and to Uncle Mike's truck. Paul's sobs and his son's cries grew louder, and when I looked over my shoulder at them, the boy's face was buried in Paul's chest.

By the time I returned to Uncle Mike and Aunt Karen's, I felt like I had been drugged. My stomach churned, and black dots were pelting everything I saw. My scalp tingled, and when I stepped out of the truck, I fell to my knees in the grass and vomited. I jammed the club back under Uncle Mike's seat and spit and wiped my mouth as I made my way inside. I remember walking in, as quiet as I could, and Uncle Mike and Aunt Karen were laughing with some of the fighters in the living room.

I got to my bedroom and shut the door, and I lay down and I don't remember how many minutes or hours passed. But I remember Aunt Karen coming to check on me. I told her I was sick.

An impenetrable sadness began filling the depths of my being, each moment deeper and worse than the last. Something inside me told me not to fight it. To let nature takes its course, whatever that meant. Days and nights combined together after that. A week felt like a few days, honestly.

I heard later through Uncle Mike that Paul was sent to the hospital. He suffered a concussion, a fractured jaw, and a broken nose and collar bone. But he never turned me in. How everyone he knew responded to that, I don't know. And I don't care. I didn't feel as bad about hitting Paul as I feel about his kid having to see it. If I knew his kid would be watching, I probably never would've done it. But I don't know.

I didn't return to Pepperdine. I had bought a cell phone over Christmas, and Ryan tried calling me on it, but I sent him a text saying my mom had died and I was dealing with that. Then, I shut my phone off. I knew he would tell Shannon we talked, and I would deal with it all later.

I didn't leave my room much, except to work out. That was the only thing that kept me sane. The gym was my outlet. But I'd always come back to my room, take a long, hot shower, slip into my sweats, and lie in my bed and let my mind relive everything from the past, the good and the bad.

When I was younger at Grandmother's, I once watched this TV show where these kids had post-traumatic stress disorder, and they would just stare off into nothingness. I always thought they were going crazy. And there were these counselors whose mission was to bring them back. But I realize now, their minds were going back and reliving the traumatic times. It was all over, they were in a place of safety, and they could go back and think. I believe it's their mind's way of digesting everything so they can put it to rest.

Uncle Mike and Aunt Karen asked what was

wrong, but I just told them I wasn't feeling good. They assumed it was about Mom, so I let them assume, and they left me alone.

I stopped shaving. The hair on my face and head grew. All I wanted to do was eat my favorite foods and end the night with a glass of whiskey I paid Tony to buy for me. I kept the bottle under my mattress. When I ate with Uncle Mike and Aunt Karen, I stayed quiet and excused myself as soon as I finished.

"How's Malibu?" guys at the dojo would ask during my workouts.

"It's all right," I said.

"How's the training going?"

"It's alright." I said that to everything. Not "good" or "bad" or anything. Just, "It's all right." When I returned home, Aunt Karen would ask, "How was your workout?"

"It was all right," I said, downing a protein shake and going back to my room. Once, Aunt Karen almost said something while she was twist-tying a sack of loaf bread, but I didn't give her the chance to.

Nightmares of Darren came and left, like short movie reels in my mind. And that image of Paul bringing the stick across Darren's neck, while the others stood and watched. Darren looking up at me and his body shaking was a continual and consistent nightmare. The visions arose not just in my bedroom, but everywhere. When I was walking down the street, when I was brushing my teeth, when I was stepping out of Uncle Mike's truck, when I was in the middle of conversations with people, everywhere and anywhere. It was exhausting.

But the nights were the worst. My thoughts would bounce from Darren to every single mistake I have ever made, every horrible thing I have ever said and did to anyone, like I was being attacked by a voice, accusing me of being this horrible person. I felt sorry for those two frat boys and Tabs' boyfriend David, whose nose I broke. I mean, I didn't have to hit them, did I? I could have just shoved them out of the way.

I remembered that Halloween party when I beat up that kid for wearing the hockey mask. I remembered the mom on the ride home, how I told her nothing would happen to her son as long as she kept it secret. And then Paul and his son's rattling cries, constantly echoing in my head.

But then, strangely, my mind would replay all the good times with Shannon. Images of the first time I saw her in New York, then again in the hotel lobby, and how beautiful she looked in Carnegie Hall. That time she leaned her back against my chest as we passed by the Statue of Liberty, the time I hovered over her in my hotel room, and all the times we spent together in Malibu, at the beach, the Christmas party when she nestled her face in my neck, and that night not long ago when she lay in my arms in my bedroom.

I pulled her yellow ribbon out of one of my books I had brought back, and laid it on the pillow beside me. Her laugh echoed in my ears. I loved and missed and hated her. I hated her for being the kind of woman I would love and be rejected by. I hated her for loving a lie—me. She was gone, and I was back in Alabama as my true self, the loser, the liar, the failure. Yep, all was back in its rightful place. I'm not fooling anyone.

Dark words screamed at me in my own voice. "You're not good enough for Shannon or anyone's love! Something's wrong with you! You had to lie about yourself to make people love you! It will not get better for you. All the good times are gone. You will die alone. Why don't you just end it all, now, and stop being a burden on everyone? We're born, we live, but we all eventually die. So why not just go out now? The pull of a trigger. That's all it'll take."

Another week passed, but I kept my phone off. After a morning workout, I stopped by my old middle school library, where I found a 1988 yearbook, the year Darren was killed. I flipped through until I found a photo of Paul, an eighth grader, probably fourteen years old at the time. I didn't recognize him as the boy he was. Our paths had never crossed back then.

Now that he wasn't wearing a mask, he wasn't a

monster anymore. He was just a kid smiling at the camera. His entire life still lay ahead of him. Then I drove to the street and sidewalk where Darren was killed. It was smaller than I remember. Though I hated that place, standing in the exact spot where it had all happened somehow brought some healing.

The next afternoon, after another workout, I was curled up in my sweats on my bed in a fetal position, staring into nothingness. Just reliving it all in front of my eyes. Then a knock came at my door. "Brian?" Uncle Mike said.

"Come in," I answered and rolled over to face him.

He stepped in and leaned against the wall. "Did something happen in California?" He's not an idiot. I knew I needed someone I trusted to confide in. He pulled the chair out from under the desk and sat in it. "What happened?" My hands held each other inside the hand warmer of my sweatshirt. I'm not sure why, but that was comforting. Seconds passed.

"Have you ever heard of a guy named Paul Turner?" I said, breaking the silence, and shifting my head so I could look at Uncle Mike.

"No."

"He's the one who killed Darren."

"How do you know?"

"He told me." Uncle Mike shifted in his seat and shook his head. I told Uncle Mike about

Paul's visit, my going to his home, hitting him, the little boy crying, everything.

Later, Uncle Mike checked in with the hospital to hear the results.

"So what are you gonna do?" Uncle Mike asked, leaning forward on his elbows.

"I've been thinking about that a lot. Paul has a wife and kid. I didn't want to admit it, but he seems like he has a really nice family. If I had killed him or turned him in for killing Darren, I'd ruin it for Paul's family. His wife and kid, they don't deserve to pay for that. But Paul ruined it for Darren. My brother could have had all those things, too."

I realized then that when we lose people we love, we don't mourn the past—we mourn unlived tomorrows. We mourn the loss of people who knew us thoroughly and loved us anyway, and we mourn the future memories that will never be made.

"And Paul took that from my brother. All that life still left. A future together. He never got to grow old and marry and have kids. I can't stand the idea of doing nothing about that."

"You said while you were hitting Paul, he just broke down in tears?" Uncle Mike asked. "Not because of the beating?"

"I don't think so," I said.

"So what caused him to break down?" I knew what Uncle Mike was doing, but I played along, because I knew I needed to. We'd get through this with the help of some psychology.

"I think he had been carrying it with him," I admitted.

"Yeah. Sounds like he's been carrying it with him his entire life. Like you," Uncle Mike said. Ouch. I felt that one go deep. Uncle Mike's never been one to pull punches.

"Are you saying he's excused?" I answered, and sat up a bit.

"No." Uncle Mike looked into his hands and rubbed them together. "If I'd accidentally killed a kid, I'd carry that with me, no matter how old I was. Especially if I couldn't tell anyone. Every day, I'd wonder what kind of man he would have become. Every day I'd wonder if this was the day someone would find out. If his parents would come to my house with the cops. And what would that do to my family? How would everyone in the neighborhood treat my family? And I'd know the victim's family would suffer and carry that with them, never finding closure. I'd never be able to live comfortably. Paul hasn't suffered on the same level as you, Brian. But don't think he hasn't suffered."

"But there's nothing I can do about it."

"Yes you can. You can forgive. That doesn't mean forgetting. Forgiveness is not letting your hate and anger rule your life. Because it will, whether you realize it or not. When you free him, you're really freeing yourself. Your forgiveness or lack of forgiveness has no effect on him."

"I still have nightmares," I said, surprised at my own admittance.

"Don't try to run from that. Give yourself permission to have those bad dreams. But don't dwell on them. Remember the good times, too. With Darren and the good times you've had since. Look at what you have in your life. There are people who still love and care about you. And you love and care about them. There are still good things you can do while you're alive. Letting Paul be with his family was one of them. And not sending him to jail for something he did when he was a kid."

"So what now?"

"The next step?"

"Yeah."

"What about creating goals and a mission for your life? Something you can be passionate about. Something only you, Brian Bailey, can do. And then give it everything you have."

"Is that what worked for you when Tommy died?"

Uncle Mike nodded. "One of my good friends was a grandfather. He used to be a therapist. And he had me imagine the doctors and nurses in a room, kneeling in front of me, begging for my forgiveness. And I took turns looking at them, one by one, saying, 'I forgive you. I forgive you for not finding the cancer sooner. I forgive you for not saving Tommy.' Doing that exercise over time helped. I never forgot what happened to Tommy. And you'll never forget what happened to Darren. But you can forgive and move on with your life. And that's the difference."

"I wonder if maybe I should have gone to counseling as a kid," I said.

"I'm sorry I didn't take you. I didn't realize you needed it. You never let on. But I should have known better. I'm sorry."

"No," I said. "It's not your fault, Uncle Mike. I wasn't saying that. I tried to forget it, and I didn't want people bringing it up. I didn't want to be anyone's pity party."

"You wouldn't have been a pity party," Uncle Mike said. "But know this. You can't run from what happened. You can't ignore it. It'll show up in short tempers. Like it has been. But if you turn around and face the bad that's happened, and embrace it as a part of what has helped mold you as a person, you can learn how to deal with it, find healing, and find peace."

I shook my head, and he continued.

"But I think that when you go back to Malibu, you should meet regularly with a counselor." I wasn't against that idea, but I didn't want to meet with a woman or any man who was too young. I wanted someone like Uncle Mike's friend, a grandfather figure.

"You want to hear something funny?" I asked. "When I was a kid, I was going to be somebody some day. And Darren would be there with me. But when he died, everything turned into a blur, like I wouldn't have much of a future."

"None of us live the life we imagined, Brian. It never turns out the way we thought it would. I didn't know Karen would have an accident, that Tommy would die, or I'd own a dojo one day. I was an officer in the Marine Corp. Leading men. I thought I'd die in battle. When we first married, we were fresh out of college. Our entire lives ahead of us. Offers to go everywhere."

"How did you move on?"

"It worked out. Just not the way we thought. At first, it's like waking up, like I'd been living in a daydream. Blind to reality. Like I'd been naive my entire life. And then I began realizing the world isn't my oyster. I can't control it. At first, it's depressing, when you realize everything's unpredictable. But later, as you accept it and grow, you realize how much freedom you have."

"Freedom?"

"Yeah. Freedom to live and learn and try new things. That's what I've been telling you and my fighters. We can't control what happens to us, but we can control how we respond. We are shaped by our past, but we are not bound by it. Remember that?"

"What about Karen? How did she handle it?"

"We chose to dwell on the good things we still had. Chose to love and be loved. We had more children after Tommy. We have two sons, actually three sons"—he winked at me—"and we're very proud of them."

Uncle Mike pointed out that in nature there are a lot of answers. He said, "There's an old sage quote. That the night is coldest and darkest just before dawn. And when the sun shines again, you get up and you get going. When the going gets tough, the tough gets going. You let the world know you're still alive. You're Brian Bailey, and you're someone to be proud of."

"But I don't know what I'm doing," I said.

And then he said something I'll never forget. "No one knows what they're doing, Brian. We just do the best we can with the knowledge we have. And that's all anyone can hope for."

That night, I had a dream that I was eight years old again. The three boys in the hockey masks stood over Darren as he lay limp on the sidewalk. Then the image changed to a white, hazy room where the walls and floor and everything around us was like an infinite white space.

Darren was beside me, sitting on a bar stool, a stool that looked like those in the photos of the pubs in Ireland. He was wearing a white t-shirt and jeans and he was barefooted. But he was healthy and pure.

Paul, as a fourteen-year-old boy, was alone and

kneeling in front of us. The hockey mask sat on top of his head, allowing us to see his face, and he looked up at us with tears streaming down his face. It was as if he was at our mercy. That we could condemn him to a life of chains if we wanted to, and that he would suffer a lot from it.

"I forgive you," Darren said to him. Shocked, I shot my eyes at Darren. Darren looked back at me, and we spoke telepathically. He said, "Now, you forgive him."

"I don't want to," I replied.

"I'm at peace," Darren answered. "Now, you forgive him, as others have forgiven you."

I looked over at Paul and he was watching me, his lip quivering, vulnerable and desperate. "I forgive you," I said. And Paul hung his head, closed his eyes, and he evaporated like a vapor. And when I looked back at Darren, he had already vanished, but it was like his smile lingered in the room.

I don't know if it was some sort of heavenly vision, or a dream because of Uncle Mike's chat with me. But I opened my eyes and it was early in the morning. Dawn had broken. Mourning doves roosted in the crape myrtles outside my window, and they were cooing back and forth in the silver light. I opened the window and the crisp air seeped in. Across the yard, I saw a squirrel sitting on a limb, looking in my direction. He churned an acorn in his hands, against his teeth. When he saw me, he stuffed the acorn in his mouth and scampered away.

My body felt weak all over, but lighter somehow. Like a weight of bricks had been taken off my shoulders. I didn't lie in bed like I had been for all those weeks, dreading getting up. I rolled out and went to the bathroom. I removed my clothes for my shower and looked in the mirror. I needed to shave, bad. So, I shaved my face, but decided to leave the hair on my head. I'm not sure why. After almost twenty years, I decided maybe it was time for a change.

My blond hair intensified the blue eyes staring back at me. I didn't remember my eyes being that blue. Something was different inside me, I could tell. I couldn't put my finger on it, but something in my face had changed. The skin under my eyes didn't look so tired anymore. I ran my fingers through my hair, and it was soft. I don't know why that surprised me.

I showered and felt the dried sweat and sleep wash off my body. I had to step out of the shower, dripping and wetting the entire bathroom floor, because I realized for the first time in my life, I needed shampoo. Aunt Karen kept some in the hall closet, so I wrapped the towel around my waist and tiptoed through the hall, leaving a trail of water drops.

I grabbed the shampoo and conditioner and jumped back into the shower. The directions said to apply and rinse, twice. So, I did. My hair felt good against my fingertips. Ruffling the hair as I shampooed it felt amazing, a sensation I've never known before.

After I finished, I slipped into my jeans and black t-shirt and entered the kitchen to the smell of bacon, eggs, and homemade biscuits. I knew it must be a Sunday because we always eat a breakfast like that on Sundays. Uncle Mike was teasing Aunt Karen. She laughed and popped him with her towel when I came in.

I felt the warmth there, the love of a family and the knowledge that those two people had been there for me all these years. They were my family. And I promised myself that I'd be there for them, too, no matter what happened today or tomorrow.

"Well, look at you," Uncle Mike said, opening the refrigerator door and pausing.

"Oh my Lord," Karen added, holding a jug of orange juice. She sat it down and walked over to me. "You have hair!" She ran her fingers through it, then she looked back at Uncle Mike, wide-eyed. "Brian, you look handsome!" she said. Uncle Mike laughed and walked over and ruffled my hair, too.

"How about that?" Uncle Mike added.

"I had hair yesterday," I said, a smile finally rising on my face. It felt good to smile again. I hadn't smiled since meeting Paul.

"Well," Aunt Karen went on, "I didn't notice it yesterday. I guess it's because you shaved." She ran her fingers over my face, a motherly touch that was comforting.

"It looks good, Brian," Uncle Mike said. "And it's good to see you smiling again."

"It sure is," Aunt Karen said, pouring three glasses of orange juice. I helped her set the table, and we all ate breakfast together, and it was the best breakfast I can ever remember.

That evening, I rode my bike back out to the pasture I used to visit all the time. I watched the sun set behind the red barn. The lightning bugs hovered, bounced, and pulsated in the spring air. Geese honked and flew in a V across the pond. A bass rolled in the water, and the crickets and bull frogs sang. The crispness in the air was invigorating as I breathed it in.

I heard a mom calling in the distance that supper was ready. Across the field, in a house, lights glowed through the windows. Two little girls, sisters perhaps, no older than seven, left their pastel-colored toys by a trampoline and ran inside. Life goes on, I thought.

I decided then that my dream was no longer to have money and success, but to be the right kind of person, to be my true self, and live the kind of life I know I can be proud of, however that's manifested. I'm going to be me and finally confess to Pepperdine who I am. So I've decided to return to California. And whatever happens, happens.

I've ordered my ticket to Los Angeles, and I leave in three days.

BB

Chapter 5

June 16, 2000

A few days ago, I turned my phone back on when I was on my way to the airport to come back to Pepperdine, and I had three voicemails from Shannon. The first one was her just checking in, the second one was her sounding frustrated, wondering why I hadn't returned her call. And then the third one was a polite message telling me she talked to Ryan, and to let her know when I was feeling better.

Shannon said she'd be there for me when I was ready to talk. I called her back and it went straight to voicemail. I left a message saying I was on the plane and I needed to meet with Dr. Daniels. I had set up a meeting with Dr. Daniels the morning after I got back. Graduation was a few days ago and there aren't as many students around. And Dr. Daniels is transitioning into the Dean of Students role. I had missed all my finals and we would need to talk about the possibility of me making them up. Hopefully, with a death in the family, all my professors will understand.

I went to the Thornton Administrative Center, the building where Dr. Daniels now has a brand new office. On the third floor, the lobby contains glass windows as walls, allowing a panoramic view of Malibu and the ocean. Chic, crème-colored carpet and fresh painted walls with wood trim at the bottom, and heavy, solid wood doors all lead into the main offices.

A secretary's desk sat on a platform in front of those big doors. If she had worn a black robe, she would have looked like a judge, peering down at me. Her hair was bobbed, her glasses sat on the end of her nose, and she wore an earpiece with a microphone.

"I'm Brian," I said. "I have an appointment with Dr. Daniels."

She checked her computer. "Yes, Mr. Bailey. Please have a seat, and I'll tell him you're here." She opened the door over her right shoulder, allowing a peek into a labyrinth of cubicles and offices. She walked in, and the door shut behind her.

I wore the best clothes I own. A black dress shirt with charcoal slacks. My black Italian leather shoes were a Christmas gift from Uncle Mike and Aunt Karen two years ago. I've only worn them twice. I hated the way I looked in the mirror, looking all pretty and high class and all, but I needed to dress well. I looked like Johnny Cash or something.

"He'll be out to see you shortly," she said, returning to her seat.

I sat on the edge of the sofa. Pepperdine alumni

magazines were stacked on an end table in an exaggerated staggered form. I bobbed my knees up and down, nervous. I took a deep breath and sank back into the sofa. I looked over at the window to all the beauty and grandeur and did something I haven't done since I was a kid. I prayed. And all I said was something I heard Grandmother say once. "Lord, let your will be done. Just don't forget me."

The door opened, and Dr. Daniels smiled and waved me in. "Come on in, Brian." He stepped toward me and shook my hand. He gave me a double-take as I crossed the threshold. "Nice hair," he said with a smile. We passed down the hall. People typed on computers and talked on phones, like something you'd see in *The Daily Planet*.

When we entered his office, it was as large as some living rooms back in Alabama. A dark oak desk, probably as heavy as a truck, sat before another glass wall with a view of the coast. A couch and two cushioned chairs encircled a coffee table with a bowl of silver-wrapped Hershey kisses and assorted chocolates.

Scents of fresh coffee lingered from a small espresso machine against the wall. Shelves held classroom books on the subjects of business administration, conflict resolution, and service leadership. I'm happy for Dr. Daniels. I hope that one day maybe I can have an office like that.

"I like your office," I said.

"Thanks. Please," he added, motioning for me to sit in one of the chairs. He sat on the couch beside me. "So, Brian," he said with a curious smile. "What can I do for you?" Wow, I thought. He just goes straight into it. I wondered if it was because he's a lot more busy now.

I leaned forward with my elbows on my knees. "I've done something kind of weird," I said. "Maybe bad. I don't want to keep on living this way without someone knowing." Dr. Daniels nodded, still waiting.

"I'm not from Ireland. I'm from Alabama, actually." I dropped the accent entirely, and a curious grin rose on his face, but he didn't say anything. He just waited. "I pretended I was from Ireland because I needed the Guinness scholarship."

He chuckled. "Go on," he said.

"Well, I came from a poor family, and I didn't qualify for grants or loans, and I wanted a better life, and I met Shannon, and Finn and Ryan . . ." I stopped there. I didn't know what all I should tell him, or what he wanted to hear. The whole thing's a really long story, and I didn't know what else to say. I confessed, which is what I came to do, and that was that. It was done.

"That's it?" he asked.

"Uh, yes, sir," I answered, perplexed.

"You faked that you were from Ireland and . . ."

he stammered, trying to make sense of it all. "Now, what did you do?" He scratched the back of his head.

"I wanted to go to school here. But I couldn't afford it. I heard about the scholarship, I learned the Irish accent, created documents that looked like the necessary documents Pepperdine wanted, and I got in." I made sure to say that the documents "looked like," rather than were "forged."

Dr. Daniels chuckled again. Then he stepped to the espresso machine, took a mug from his desk, and poured coffee into it. "So, that's it?" he answered.

"Yes, sir," I said.

"You want some?" he asked, pointing at the coffee.

"No, sir. Thank you."

"I thought you were going to tell me you burned down your kitchen or something. When Finn called, he said to take it easy on you, and he made it sound catastrophic."

"Finn called you?"

"Yeah. He was on his way to Kenya. He said you had something really important to confess, and that we should take it easy on you. And to remember Pepperdine's motto: Freely give as you have freely received. He said you were a good guy, that you had grown up a lot, and that you had a rough background, but you were turning around. He said you were becoming the kind of person Pepperdine would be proud of. He also told me about what you did for Tabitha."

Then Dr. Daniels looked at me with a satisfied smile. "It's great what you did, going up and saving a friend like that. She could have died." I didn't say anything. "In my line of work, you hear all kinds of things."

Dr. Daniels sat down and adjusted his tie. "I've been a professor here for over fifteen years, serving on boards, all those things. And this Ireland story, you coming from Alabama, studying theology, of all subjects, sleeping in the library, your classmates and professors caring about you, rescuing a girl at a party, that's one for the books, kid."

Then he got real serious and even pointed a finger at me. "But don't misunderstand me. I'm not advocating that you lie, and I'm not saying what you did is okay." He was looking at me like Uncle Mike does at times. "But, knowing a bit of your background, I understand why you did it. But we'll have to tell the committee."

"Committee?"

"Student Affairs. And they may bring you in for some questions. I don't know what they'll say or do, but I'll do what I can for you. Okay? I'll draft up a letter for your professors, letting them know you had a death in the family, and asking permission to let you take your finals."

"Thank you."

"You're welcome."

"Do you think I'll go to jail?" I asked, standing.

"Jail?! No," he said, standing and chuckling. "They might not let you go to school here anymore, but this doesn't warrant jail. Your confessing helps, and like I said, I'll do what I can."

"Thank you," I said again, and we shook hands. "I really do love it here. This place has changed my life."

"I know it has, Brian," he said, smiling. "It's that way for a lot of us."

"And I'll take my punishment," I continued. "But if there's any way I can stay as an American student, I want to. I'll do whatever I need to do to make this right."

"I know you will, Brian," he said, patting my back as he ushered me to his door. "We'll be in touch." Then he opened the door for me, and smiled goodbye.

When I left, the secretaries and people in their cubicles still pounded at their keyboards and talked away. Sirens didn't squeal. The police didn't flood campus to get me. I wasn't escorted off the premises. I just stepped outside into the courtyard. The sun warmed my face, and the light breeze felt good as it lifted my hair and fanned my cheek. I could hear the ceaseless motion of the waves as they rolled and crashed in the distance. I feel a lot better about myself. It feels good to be honest. A part of me wishes I confessed the truth sooner.

Tonight, I stood at our living room window, watching the lights flicker along the coast and the moon's trail along the waters. I dread Pepperdine's verdict. Some on the board might think my story's cute, but they still have to make decisions for the integrity of the university. They can't let students lie and get away with it.

I thought about Shannon. I miss her company terribly. Our talks, her laugh, that moment on my bed before going home on our last night together. I can't stop thinking about touching her cheek and tucking her lock of hair behind her ear. Our faces near each other's. The warmth of her breath on my lips.

All these years I haven't let many people in. I didn't trust them. The people I should have been able to depend on the most as a kid had never been there. All I've ever wanted was for people to know the good and the bad in me, and still want to be my friend. I hoped I'd meet a girl like Shannon who'd say, "I'm not perfect, either. But our love can be perfect—by staying committed to each other, forever, no matter what comes our way."

I want to be myself and only myself, and not pretend to be anyone else anymore. I'm beginning to like me, and I haven't felt that way since I was a kid.

Shannon called after I left her a voicemail, and we talked a while. She wanted to talk about my mom, and we did. Shannon did her best to console me, but I didn't need consoling. She wants to get together and talk in person, but I told her I'm not ready yet. I need a few days to prepare to face the committee, and I don't want to be distracted. I explained that to her, and she understood. At least I hope she did.

BB

June 22, 2000

The committee made a decision, and I would write about the meeting in detail, but there's not much to say.

I thought I'd be nervous, but I wasn't. I guess it's because I had already accepted the fact that I would take whatever punishment they decided. I was at peace, I think, because I knew that if I had to do it over, I wouldn't change anything. I'm not proud of lying to anyone, but if I hadn't come to Pepperdine, I would never have met Finn, Ryan, Tabs, Joanna, Matt or Patrick, and my relationship with Shannon would've dissipated.

Nothing in my life has turned out the way I imagined it would. But I'm all right now, because I know I love a woman and she loves me. And I have a family, Uncle Mike and Aunt Karen, and I have a few good friends. From now on, I want to spend more time dwelling on the good in my life, rather than on what I've lost.

So three days ago, in the Thornton Administrative Center, I stood before seven men in business suits sitting in black swivel chairs. Dr. Daniels was there. They sat along a polished oak table, flipping through a file in front of them. The file was about me. Highlights a secretary thought best to include, I guess. I saw my photo on a cover sheet in one of the folders.

Each of those men wore politician attire, and all had either white or salt-and-pepper hair. Clean-shaven faces. Some wore trendy glasses, others wore grandpa glasses. None of those men looked dumb, though. They were sharp, and very intelligent, and like Uncle Mike, had probably seen and heard everything.

I knew I wouldn't be able to fool those guys. Complete and utter honesty was my best ally. So I told them the entire story, the story I've recorded in my journal, and I told them I was sorry I deceived everyone.

When they realized I hadn't created fake documents, but that I had created documents that looked like fake documents, it changed the climate of the room. At one point, Dr. Daniels told the men that I had been treated like a younger brother by Finn and Ryan. All the men knew those two, and so that went over well. My professors had turned in good reports about me, and my academic standing was good. Not excellent, but good.

"I made my bed," I told them. "I'll take my punishment. Whatever you decide to do, I'll accept it. But I don't want to leave Pepperdine. If it's possible, I'd like to stay. Because I love it here."

"It's the first place that's ever felt like a home to you, isn't it?" asked one of the men.

And I realized then that some of them were understanding me. All I could do was nod. That question surprised me.

In the end, they said they'd make a decision and get back to me in a few days. When I was dismissed, I nodded and said thank you, and I left without saying anything to Dr. Daniels. I didn't want to leave the impression that we were buddies or that I had an inside man.

Earlier today, Dr. Daniels called me. He said the board was taking away my Os Guinness Scholarship, and that I'll have to pay it back. All of it. But there's a faculty/staff scholarship they give to students who've messed up. It's called the Scholarship of Second Chances. It's for students who had to leave Pepperdine because of drugs or crimes, and who want to come back. It's actually more of a loan—the deal is, after you graduate, you have to contribute a part of your income back to the scholarship until it's paid in full.

They talked to my professors. They said everyone liked me and that I was hard working. As long as I maintain a C average, the scholarship will cover half my tuition. Pepperdine will grant me student loans.

So I didn't get kicked out! When Dr. Daniels explained it to me, I started jumping up and down, and punching the air. "Yes! Thank you! Thank you so much!"

Then Dr. Daniels said something I'll never forget. "You're welcome," he said. "There are a lot of people around here who've seen the good in you, and they all agree you've got a lot of potential. It looks like you've made an impact on some people here. The state of Alabama would be proud of you. You and Finn have represented the South well. There are a few documents you'll need to sign, and we'll need your real ID and records, but that's it."

When we hung up, I wrote Uncle Mike and Aunt Karen and told them everything. I told them for the first time about going to school at Pepperdine, confessing, and the board giving me a break. I got an email from them a few minutes ago and they said they were proud of me, and thankful to learn the truth, but not to lie to them again. I know I won't.

I applied for a job as a waiter at Coogie's and was accepted. It'll be fun, I think. I've seen famous people there. Pamela Anderson, Ted Danson,

John Cusack, and Dick Van Dyke, at different times. Ted Danson was just sipping coffee reading a newspaper the other day. Pamela Anderson was decked out in a white blouse, white jeans, white shoes, and black sunglasses.

With wages and tips, and since they let us eat there for free during our shifts, I believe I can make it work. I can only take three classes at Pepperdine per semester, but that's fine because I get to stay in school! I don't have to be from Ireland and lie anymore, and Ryan said I can keep staying here at the apartment with him.

BB

June 25, 2000

Two days ago, I decided to tell Shannon the entire story about Darren, all the details of how I came to Pepperdine, everything.

So, I left my journal on her doorstep. I also returned her yellow ribbon. I stuck it in the middle of the journal so it wouldn't blow away. And I left this note attached:

Dear Shannon,
This is my journal. It will tell you everything. I've kept your ribbon with me ever since New York, because I wanted to keep a part of you with me. I hope you don't mind. You said that one day you hoped I would write our story, that I would write

about you. Now, as you read this journal, you will know that your part in my story will be the most beautiful part. I want you to know that no matter what happens today or tomorrow, I'm okay with it, I'm at peace, because I know I love you. I believe everything in my life has led me to you. My choices, the circumstances, both the good and the bad. When we're together, the journey feels worth it. Because if anything had happened differently in my life, I would never have received the gift of knowing and loving you.

—Brian

Yesterday, I was lying on my bed, thinking about Shannon, and I heard a knock on the apartment door. When I opened it, she was standing there, wearing a gentle smile, and that made me feel good. Because I knew she was at peace. She was holding my journal and her ribbon was inside it, poking out at the top. Her eyes scanned my hair and she bit back a smile.

"I looked everywhere for this after New York," she said, glancing down and fingering the ribbon. I guess now wasn't the time to talk about hairstyles. She stared into my eyes for a moment, then she just stepped toward me and hugged me, and it was soft and warm.

When she let go, my heart started pounding, and

my knees felt numb, because I wasn't sure what she was going to say next. She had the power to crush me into a million pieces, and that's a beautiful vulnerability I wouldn't exchange for anything.

I had to sit because my knees were weak, so I invited her in, and we sat on the couch. She sat beside me, and my heart was pounding so hard I thought it was going to burst through my ribcage. She didn't start saying, "I've given this some thought, and it's not going to be easy for me to say this, but" or something along those lines.

Instead, she just sat there with this expectant look on her face, waiting for me to talk.

"You don't want to talk about anything in the journal?" I asked.

"I have some questions," she said. "But they can wait."

I thought I'd ask if she read about Darren, and if she now realizes how crazy I am, and all the things that would come with that. But this time, when I opened my mouth to speak, strange emotions took over, and I felt a tingling in my cheeks and a choking in my throat. Those were sensations I hadn't felt since I was eight years old.

I stopped for a moment, blinked away the water that rose behind my eyes, and I swallowed hard. I glanced up at her, and her eyes weren't blinking. They were locked on mine, like she was astonished. I guess she wasn't expecting me to get emotional.

I never thought I'd feel anything real again for anyone. But sitting there with her, given our past, and how lovely those memories and feelings were, I was completely at her mercy. And there was nothing I could do about it. I was laid bare.

I cleared my throat, trying to get rid of that awful lump that kept rising. I shifted in my seat, trying to keep cool. "You read it?" I asked, finally, without the choked whispers.

Shannon nodded.

"The whole thing?" I asked.

She nodded again.

"I read it in one sitting," she said. "Why did you tell them the truth?"

"Who?"

"The committee."

"I just didn't want to lie anymore. I'm tired," I said, surprised at my comment. I didn't even realize I was tired of lying until those words came out. Then, my lip quivered.

"Just tell me the truth," she said, taking my hands in hers. "That's all I ever want to hear, just the truth. Be open and honest with me. Always."

"I'm sorry about keeping your ribbon," I said, nodding, letting her know I heard her. "I just wanted to keep a part of you with me." I had regained my senses now. The emotions had settled. And Shannon chuckled, like my apology wasn't necessary. But I wasn't laughing. I still didn't know how this was all going to end.

"I love you," she said, and I knew she meant it as more than just a friend.

Those emotions I had kept in check tried to erupt, and all these strange sensations filled my entire body. I don't know what they are or what they're called. I shot out of my chair and rushed to the door, then I turned back around and grabbed my temples with my hand. My nose tingled horribly and some heavy tears spilled over my eyes, which I quickly wiped. I was embarrassed.

Her words scared me because no one had ever told me they loved me before. I didn't know exactly what she meant, either. And that scared me, too. What if I read too much into it? What if later, she regretted saying that because she didn't mean it? Because, you know, maybe she was just caught up in the moment.

I can't handle someone leaving my life again. That's all it seems people do in my life. Just come, make me love them, and leave.

Shannon stared at me, wide-eyed, and then, as if coming to herself, she blinked her soft eyes and walked over to me. When my back hit the door, she drew closer. She took my hands, and pulled them down to our waists. Then, she wrapped her arms around me and kissed my lips and whispered, "I love you."

I hid my face in my hand, squeezing my temples harder, trying to hold the emotions back, trying not to break down. I refused to look her in the eyes. I knew I'd fall apart if I did. She pulled my hand away from my face, making me look at her. "I love you," she whispered again.

"Don't say it unless you mean it," I muttered, coughing and huffing through the tears. They were pouring out like a steady stream now. "I can't lose someone again."

"I'm not going anywhere," she said. "Because I love you."

Then, something inside me broke like a bow that had been bending over the years and finally had the relief of snapping. I buried my face into her neck, and I wept.

It was humiliating, humbling, and wonderful all at once.

BB

July 28, 2007
7 years later
College was the most amazing, exciting, and the wildest ride of my life. I learned lessons and made friends that'll last me a lifetime. I wouldn't change anything, not even the hard times. It was the best of times and the worst of times, but it was our time. And I grew more in those four years than I have before or ever have since.

Shannon and I married after I graduated. She teaches full-time at Pepperdine now. Her acting never went anywhere, but when a minor position calls for it, she'll act in plays she directs. She refuses to play major roles, leaving those for her students instead.

Every other week, I meet with a counselor, a grandfather figure named Dr. Cates. He's on staff at Pepperdine and they provide free counseling to students, faculty, and staff. He's helping me work through the past with Darren and my mom.

For the last two years, I've been volunteering as a tutor every Thursday night at Camp David Gonzales in Calabasas. It's a center where at-risk kids under eighteen are sent to live and learn that there's a different life outside the neighborhoods where they grew up. I help the boys with their homework and talk to them about the only life they've ever known. I tell them my story, and I can tell it helps. But they've helped me more than I've helped them.

After I graduated with a bachelor's in psychology, I was awarded a full-time job in the study abroad office. I now oversee the programs in the U.K. and Italy. I even created a study abroad program in Ireland. No kidding. I counsel and advise students as they make those international transitions. They leave as kids and always return a bit more mature, a bit sharper. Shannon and I travel to Ireland, England and Italy every other year to visit the programs. And Pepperdine pays for it. That's nice.

Since Shannon and I are both faculty and staff,

we get free apartment housing on campus. Shannon was debt-free when we got married, and it didn't take us long to pay back the Os Guinness Scholarship. I've even enrolled in Pepperdine's master's program in counseling. Since I'm an employee, I get a 75% off my tuition. One day, I plan to get my license and open my own counseling practice, just as I said I would.

With Shannon, we strive to place each other's desires and needs above our own, and always express unconditional respect and love. And we've agreed that no matter what happens, we'll be committed to each other. At the end of the day, that's what counts. You just have to be committed.

Marriage isn't easy, of course. We have our disagreements, but we're happy. When we fight, we try to remind ourselves that the other is a good person, that we love each other, and the bad times will pass.

Our dining room wall is made mostly of glass and allows us to peer out across the balcony and coast. During the week, we wake up an hour earlier than we should, just so we can have breakfast and coffee together.

There, we watch the bumblebees and honey-bees chase each other among the lilies. The air is always filled with the scent of ocean salt and flowers. Songs from seagulls echo in the ravines that lead up to our back door.

Emerald green–backed hummingbirds fuss with

the yellow-headed orioles over who gets to drink the nectar from the violet and sugar-yellow perennials planted across the hillsides. They chatter and squawk and look behind them as they fly away. In the evenings, the swallows dart and dive in the air, their bodies and wings silhouetted against the sunsets over the crashing waves.

Shannon and I go for walks and talks together on campus and at the beach. Those walks and talks have been great for us. We try to eat dinner on the balcony in the evenings, watch the tangerine sunset evolve into a star-filled sky. We don't own a TV. We don't need one.

Uncle Mike, Aunt Karen, and Shannon's parents visit us every summer. They use the trips as a vacation. They love it here. We have a guest bedroom for them, but we rent it out to a student in the spring and fall. That's extra income for groceries and whatnot. Shannon's mom has to walk with a cane, but she manages. We spend our Thanksgivings in Alabama and our Christmases in Nor Cal.

I still see Finn and Ryan at homecomings, but not the others as much. A few years after Finn left Pepperdine, he wrote a memoir called *The Mason Jar*, which details his love affair with Eden and what happened with her. *The Mason Jar* became a best-seller, and there's even talk that it'll be turned into a feature film. I'd tell you what happened with Eden, but I'd ruin the story.

Finn's work is what inspired me to turn my journals into my own memoir. But mine won't be as good as his, no matter what he'll tell me later.

As I look back on my journey thus far, if I could say anything to my readers, I'd say that to know who you are, you must forget who people tell you to be. The greatest feat of courage is when we decide to live as our true selves, despite the condescending attitude from others.

And there will always be people who will take advantage of the real you. And their reasons for doing so will vary. They'll make fun of you, talk about you when you're not around, make assumptions and judgments grounded on speculation rather than truth. So, you might as well go about doing what you know is right and good. Because they'll have their opinions, no matter what.

That's the risk in being vulnerable. But those people who don't know you, they don't love you. So why care about their opinions? The people who love you, the real you, will know you. And that's what makes vulnerability worth it. If you can count on your hand the number of people who will be there for you through anything, you're a wealthy person.

In this life, we shouldn't look for someone who will fix us or solve our problems. We need to be with people who help us want to become better, and who will stand, walk, and crawl with us during our times of pain and loss. And they'll know that we would do the same for them.

What do Shannon and I do these days when we're not working? Well, we try to enjoy life, just like everybody else, and live it each day at a time.

This morning was Shannon's and my three year wedding anniversary. Yesterday, I wrote this to her in a card:

Dear Shannon,
I know now that one of the reasons I fell in love with you is because I had seen a lot of ugly. And you were beautiful. You taught me that I could be myself and still be loved. Every time I revealed more of my true self to you, you stepped closer to me, not away.

You saved my life with your love. You made me want to be a better person. You gave me reasons to live, to love and forgive, and to become the best version of myself. I often wonder if you know how much you mean to me and the difference you've made in my life. If I ever lost you, I know I will have lost a sacred treasure, which I know I'll never find again.

I love you,
Brian

It's raining outside, right now. It's foggy. The wood in the fireplace is now ash and coals, because last night, we ate dinner there, celebrating our anniversary. The scents of burned oak linger in the room. Deep down, those coals burn hot. A small flame poked its head up between the larger embers, so I stoked it and added three more logs to get the fire going again.

We made love by that fire last night, murmuring words of affection and appreciation to each other between caresses and kisses. Then, I traced her skin with my fingertips while we watched the flames curl around the wood. And she fell asleep in my arms. Later, I picked her up and carried her to bed. She woke me this morning, and we made love again.

I make it a point to tell her I love her every day. In the mornings, at lunchtime, when we return from work, and even when we meet each other in a room after being gone a few hours. We hug, and we whisper, "I love you."

Once when the fire was snapping and popping, and the wood aflame, I went into the kitchen to check on her. She was humming with her back turned to me, making biscuits from scratch. Her fingers were caked with dough. I had just taken a shower, and I was wearing nothing but my jeans. My hair was still damp.

I took in the sight of her and the pink sky through the window, still holding traces of the sunrise. She had slipped into my crisp white dress shirt, which she'd picked up from the bedroom floor. I could see the curves in her calves and thighs, and she had rolled my sleeves up. My shirt swallowed her whole. You never realize how small a woman is until she wears your clothes. She mashed the biscuit dough into the cooking sheet on the counter, making palm-sized silver dollars. Then she slid a pan of biscuits into the oven.

I moved behind her and wrapped my arms around her waist and kissed her neck. She hopped a little, and giggled. She craned her neck around and her lips met mine. She held her hands up and away to keep the dough from getting on me. Some of the flour still got in my hair, but I didn't care.

I turned her around and lifted her onto the counter, because we didn't have to be anywhere anytime soon. I was in that moment with her. I'm her husband. She's my wife. I am hers, and she is mine. I stay in the here and now. Tomorrow will take care of itself, and today will be well spent.

I have no idea what will happen in the future. But I know this, right now. I know who I am. I know where I've been and I know where I'm going. My name is Brian Oz Bailey. And my life hasn't turned out any way I ever imagined it would. But I couldn't be happier.

Center Point Large Print
600 Brooks Road / PO Box 1
Thorndike, ME 04986-0001 USA

(207) 568-3717

US & Canada:
1 800 929-9108
www.centerpointlargeprint.com